FOG AND O[...]

LATCHMERE JUNIOR SCHOOL
LATCHMERE ROAD
KINGSTON UPON THAMES
SURREY
KT2 5TT

The *Oxford Progressive English Readers* series provides a wide range of reading for learners of English.

Each book in the series has been written to follow the strict guidelines of a syllabus, wordlist and structure list. The texts are graded according to these guidelines; Grade 1 at a 1,400 word level, Grade 2 at a 2,100 word level, Grade 3 at a 3,100 word level, Grade 4 at a 3,700 word level and Grade 5 at a 5,000 word level.

The latest methods of text analysis, using specially designed software, ensure that readability is carefully controlled at every level. Any new words which are vital to the mood and style of the story are explained within the text, and reoccur throughout for maximum reinforcement. New language items are also clarified by attractive illustrations.

Each book has a short section containing carefully graded exercises and controlled activities, which test both global and specific understanding.

Fog and Other Stories

Bill Lowe

Hong Kong
Oxford University Press
Oxford Singapore Tokyo

Oxford University Press

Oxford　New York　Toronto
Kuala Lumpur　Singapore　Hong Kong　Tokyo
Delhi　Bombay　Calcutta　Madras　Karachi
Nairobi　Dar es Salaam　Cape Town
Melbourne　Auckland　Madrid

and associated companies in
Berlin　Ibadan

Oxford is a trade mark of Oxford University Press

First published 1992
Third impression 1994

© Oxford University Press 1992

All rights reserved. No part of this publication may be reproduced,
stored in a retrieval system, or transmitted, in any form or by any means,
without the prior permission in writing of Oxford University Press
(Hong Kong) Ltd. Within Hong Kong, exceptions are allowed in respect
of any fair dealing for the purpose of research or private study,
or criticism or review, as permitted under the Copyright Ordinance
currently in force. Enquiries concerning reproduction outside
these terms and in other countries should be sent to
Oxford University Press (Hong Kong) Ltd at the address below

This book is sold subject to the condition that it shall not, by way of
trade or otherwise, be lent, re-sold, hired out or otherwise circulated
without the publisher's prior consent in any form of binding or cover
other than that in which it is published and without a similar condition
including this condition being imposed on the subsequent purchaser

Illustrated by K.Y. Chan

Syllabus designer: David Foulds

Text processing and analysis by Luxfield Consultants Ltd.

ISBN 0 19 585397 0

Printed in Hong Kong
Published by Oxford University Press (Hong Kong) Ltd
18/F Warwick House, Taikoo Place, 979 King's Road,
Quarry Bay, Hong Kong

Contents

1 Fog 1
2 Time and Place 16
3 The Loan 22
4 The Truth 40
5 Taxi 47
6 The Party 62
7 The Vase 69
   Questions and Activities 85

Fog

Polly leaves work early

Polly looked out of the office window at the people hurrying along the busy London street. The people were all dressed in thick winter coats. Their hands were in their pockets. They did not stop at the brightly lit shop windows. They were all in a hurry to get home.

Polly looked at her own warm coat hanging at the back of the door, then at the clock. It was five minutes to four. In another five minutes she could join the people in the street. Usually she did not finish work until five o'clock, but like most of the workers in London, she would leave earlier today.

When she had left home at eight o'clock that morning, the city had been covered in a grey mist. The weather report on the radio had told Londoners that it would be a bad day: the mist was expected to get thicker. At lunchtime the weatherman had advised listeners to leave work early: by evening the mist would become a thick fog.

Londoners sometimes call such a fog 'a pea-souper' for it looks as thick as pea soup. In such conditions no buses, trains, or cars can run, and even short journeys on foot become almost impossible.

The office manager put his head round the door, 'You had better go now Polly, it's getting quite thick.' She put the cover on her typewriter. Then she crossed the room to where her coat hung, took a comb from her pocket and looked into the small mirror on the wall.

'Nobody is going to see whether my hair is tidy or not on a night like this,' she thought.

Satisfied with her appearance, she put on the warm winter coat that her father had given her for Christmas. She buttoned the collar tightly around her neck, and left the office, locking the door behind her.

In the outside office she handed the keys to the girl at the telephone desk. 'I'm glad that I only live a few minutes' walk away,' said the girl. 'How far do you have to go, Polly?'

'Usually it takes me about an hour,' Polly replied, 'but tonight it's going to take a lot longer.'

'I hope you can catch a bus,' said the other girl. 'I'd hate to have to walk through the streets in this weather.'

'I'll manage,' smiled Polly. 'See you tomorrow. Good night.'

No buses to Crouch End

Out in the street Polly walked towards her usual bus stop. A long line of people stood waiting there. At the end of the line stood a bus inspector. 'How far are you going?' he asked as Polly joined the line.

'Crouch End,' said Polly.

Crouch End is a quiet part of north London. Polly lived there with her parents in Garden Road, a very pleasant, tree-lined road where each of the houses had its own little garden. It was a nice place to live, and usually it was easy to get to from central London.

'Sorry, miss,' said the bus company man, 'but the buses are not going as far as that. The fog is too thick. If you want my advice you'll take an Underground train to Finsbury Park. The fog may not be so bad out there and you might get a taxi.'

The Underground trains did not go as far as Crouch End, and Finsbury Park was two miles from Polly's home.

Polly looked around her. More people were already making their way to the Underground station. There was no time to stand and think, she had to decide what to do! The fog was too thick to see more than a few yards along the road. As people passed her they became grey shadows and disappeared a few seconds later.

As she stood on the moving stairs in the Underground station Polly thought that she should have telephoned home. Her parents would be worried about her. But it was too late to turn back now. She would call them from Finsbury Park.

As she stood in the crowd of people who were all waiting for the train, she had the feeling that she was being watched. A few feet away from her a tall man in a dark coat had his eyes fixed on her. She looked straight at him, and he turned his head away. Usually she gave no thought to such things, for she was used to this kind of attention.

A crowded train

The train arrived and the waiting crowd moved forward. Tonight, with so many people leaving their work early, and with the buses not running, the trains were more crowded than usual. Polly was amongst the last few people to get into the train. There were about fifty people standing around her, all squeezed tightly into a small space.

Soon her thoughts were lost in the sound of the train, that sound that goes on and on and which sends so many travellers to sleep.

When the train stopped at the first station, the sudden movement threw Polly against the woman in front of her.

The person behind pressed close to Polly's back. The doors of the train opened and, as people started to push towards them, Polly noticed again the tall man in the dark coat. He was still watching her.

A few people got off the train, but many more got on. Polly began to feel sorry that she had decided to make this journey by train. It was going to be an uncomfortable ride home. 'Twelve more stations to go,' she thought. If there were no taxis at Finsbury Park she would have a two-mile walk from there.

She thought of the fog outside and felt glad that she knew the road well between the station and her home. She had often walked there and back home again on a bright, sunny Sunday morning. She felt sure that she could find her way, even in a thick fog.

The train moved from side to side as it sped on its way from station to station. The tall man was behind her now and Polly had the uncomfortable feeling that his eyes were always on her. She began to feel a little frightened and looked around to see if there was anyone in the train that she knew. Comforting herself she thought that,

Polly phones home

At last the train arrived at Finsbury Park station. Polly turned to reach the door. As the people moved out she looked at the faces around her. There was still nobody that she knew, but the tall man had gone. Polly hoped that he had left the train at an earlier station. Then she saw him a little way in front of her on the moving stairs, but when she reached the top of the stairs he was out of sight.

The smell of the fog hit her nose. There were fewer people now. She walked to the telephone at the station entrance.

The telephone was being used. She waited. People passed by her, disappearing into the thick grey fog outside. The man using the telephone talked on. 'Well I can't get home tonight,' he was saying. 'This fog is too thick! I can't see my own hand in front of me.'

Two minutes later the station entrance was empty. Outside, the fog lay like a thick grey cloud. At last the man put down the telephone, 'Sorry to keep you waiting, Miss.'

A minute later Polly was speaking to her mother. 'Polly, are you all right dear?' Her mother's voice sounded warm and comforting. 'Your father telephoned a few minutes ago. He's had to leave the car, the fog is much too thick for him to drive. Yes dear, like you, your father is going to walk home. Try not to get lost, and call again if you pass a telephone on your way.'

Polly told her mother that she would be all right. She did not want her to know that she felt frightened. She looked out into the street and thought again of the tall man. She could see no one.

Footsteps

Putting down the telephone she started off in the direction of the main road. All the shops were closed, but a few of them had left window lights on. Polly tried to move from one light to the next, but it was difficult.

One of the biggest problems of moving through a really thick fog is that light does not shine through it very far. The lights from the shop windows only made small circles of light.

Polly moved slowly forward, entering a small circle of light for a few seconds, and then being swallowed up again in a world of complete darkness.

She thought of the words spoken by the man on the telephone, 'I can't see my own hand in front of me.' With a strange feeling of fear mixed with excitement she held up her hand. It was a little more than twelve inches from her face. She couldn't see it!

She could hear footsteps, but were they in front of her, behind her, or away to her left? She could not say. She stretched out her right hand and touched a shop window. She held her left hand in front of her, slowly feeling her way along like a blind person.

She reached the corner. The footsteps had gone. She could hear voices but could not tell if they were near or shouting from a long way off. Now she had to turn left and cross the road. The light from the window of the corner shop showed only halfway across the pavement.After that there was only darkness, and fog. She moved out, feeling with her foot for the step down into the road.

Suddenly there was a movement. A rough hand brushed her face and a man's voice sounded in her ear, 'Sorry, Miss.' The man moved off towards the corner shop. Polly stood quite still for a few seconds. She could hear her heart beating with fright. The man's sudden appearance had surprised her. She did not think it was funny, but she could not help giving a little laugh when she thought that she may have frightened him too.

Now she was in the road. At least she did not have to think about the traffic; there was none. Halfway across she felt unsure of her direction. 'Don't turn round,' she told herself, 'try to go straight.' She began to walk more surely. In the middle of the road there was nothing to bump into. She listened for the sound of footsteps or voices. She saw a small light trying to break through the fog. She went towards it.

Her foot hit the step and she was thrown to the ground. She had not known that she was so close to the pavement on the other side of the road. There were tears in her eyes as she got to her feet. Her hand went down to her knee. Her stockings were torn and she could feel blood beneath her fingers.

A friendly voice

Moving into the light of the shop window, she examined her leg. Luckily it was not very bad. She had dropped her handbag as she had fallen and began looking around for it. It was not in the circle of light. Carefully she moved out of the light. She could not see the ground at her feet. Her foot hit something and she bent down to feel what it was. Her fingers touched the familiar surface. Picking up her bag she moved back into the light. Everything in the bag was there. She took out a handkerchief and dried her eyes.

For a few minutes she stood by the shop window resting. She knew the shop and therefore knew that she was going in the right direction. She was in the main road now. There were more shops and so more lights. She could move slowly from one light to the next.

As she started off she heard the sound of footsteps coming towards her. A dark shape appeared. Polly stopped. A woman's voice said, 'Terrible isn't it, dear? Go carefully.' It was a friendly sound, a motherly voice. It made Polly feel better.

There were more people about in the main road. She could hear the sound of other voices coming to her out of the darkness. She moved along more easily, and as she passed out of each circle of light her fingers reached out for the building beside her. Touching the wall, she felt her way along.

In the light of a shop window she looked at her watch; it was nearly five-thirty. As she walked forwards, slowly and carefully, she tried to work out how long it would take her to get home. If normal walking speed was about three miles an hour, she could only hope to move at one mile an hour in this fog. She had two miles to walk.

Is someone following?

Her thoughts were stopped by the sound of footsteps. She thought the sound came from behind her. She had just passed out of a circle of light, and she looked back into it, her eyes trying hard to see any sort of movement. For a second she thought that she saw someone — the tall man? She could not be sure. It seemed as if someone had stepped to one side into a shop doorway. She stood quite still, listening. The footsteps had stopped.

Maybe she had imagined it. A minute later she heard the steps again. This time she did not stop to look back. She told herself that it was foolish to let her fears play tricks on her.

More people passed her, walking in ones and twos, moving like blind people through the darkness. Her thoughts then made her smile. Science has made it possible for people to fly to the moon. We can pick up a telephone and speak to someone on the other side of the world. We can do so many wonderful things, but the weather still controls us. A thick fog can bring a great city to a complete stop.

Several times during the next hour she heard footsteps behind her. They were not always there, but when she heard them her mind went back to the tall man on the train. There had been something unpleasant about the way that he had watched her. She told herself that she should not imagine things, but the bad thoughts refused to go away. Once or twice when she had heard the footsteps, she had stopped to listen. Each time she had done so there had been silence. Then, as she moved forward again she heard someone moving along slowly behind her.

Trying not to be afraid, Polly told herself that there might be someone walking in front of her who was feeling afraid when they heard her own footsteps.

She looked again at her watch. This would be the last shop window — she was now moving into streets where there were no shops. It would be more difficult now, no light at all except for the few street lamps that were set far apart from one another. It was after six-thirty.

Reaching the corner she managed to cross the wide road in front of her. On the other side her hand found the garden wall of the house on the corner. Slowly she moved round the corner into the smaller side-street. There was only one more main crossing and then it would be all small roads. She knew all these roads very well, but there would be few people about and no lights at all.

Lost

Polly was beginning to feel cold and hungry. The bright comfort of her office seemed like another world. Was it only two and a half hours ago that she had left it? It seemed like a far-off memory. If only someone that she knew would come along, someone to talk to.

Her slow movement through this silent darkness was wearing her down. Slow step after slow step — if only she could move faster!

She stopped again, listening. There were no footsteps, the silence was complete. It was as if the whole world had died around her. Could she be sure of her own knowledge of the streets? She had only this and her touch to tell her which way to go. What if she had been wrong? What if she was in the wrong street? Wild thoughts flew through her head. What if she was lost and nobody came along? What would happen if she could not find her way home? Suddenly she was crying with fear. She wanted to shout out but no sound came.

With tears running down her face, Polly kept moving slowly forward, unsure, frightened, but not stopping for more than a second. She almost wished that she could hear the footsteps again.

Reaching the next corner she went into the road. She kept stretching her foot forward, feeling for the pavement on the other side. Had she moved up onto the pavement without knowing it? Her hands reached out trying to touch the wall. Unsure of herself she turned around. Now she did not know which way she was facing. Was she in the middle of the road?

She spoke aloud to herself, 'This is stupid! I know this road so well.'

Then she heard it — a soft footstep. Then a cough, a deep sound. She stood quite still, trying to be sure about the direction of the sound. It was on her left, and it was getting nearer. A minute before she had been wishing for someone to come along. Now she wanted to run, but fear held her still. The footsteps were quite close. Then she heard another sound from the same direction, a strange tapping noise.

The helpful stranger

She heard the cough again, this time it could not have been more than three or four yards away. The footsteps stopped suddenly. A man's voice came from out of the darkness, 'Is anybody there?' It was a deep voice, not the voice of a young man.

Polly told herself that this was what she wanted, for someone to come along. At last she spoke, 'Hello, I think I'm lost.' There was a second's silence, then a soft laugh, then the footsteps moved towards her.

A few seconds later a hand reached out and touched her arm. Polly found herself looking up at a tall man who stood with his hand still resting on her arm. It was not the man from the train. The face that looked down on her was that of an older man.

'I've no doubt that there are many people lost tonight, my dear. Where are you going? Maybe I can help you.'

'If you could just tell me where I am,' said Polly.

'I'm not sure of the name of this road,' replied the man, 'but I know it well enough. Which road do you want?'

'I live in Garden Road. Am I anywhere near it?'

Again the man laughed softly, as if, thought Polly, he was enjoying a joke to himself.

'Just take my hand,' said the man. 'Come with me my dear, you'll be all right.'

Polly could not think clearly. Should she go with him? He had not answered her question. 'Do you know Garden Road?' she asked.

'Yes I know it well,' he replied. 'Come along my dear, you don't want to stay out in this fog any longer than you need to.' He took Polly's hand and pulled her towards him. 'Watch out for the step here.'

'Don't worry'

In his other hand the man carried a stick. Polly heard it hit the step. That was the tapping sound that she had heard: his stick hitting the road. 'It was very wise of you to bring a stick out with you,' she said.

'Yes it makes it easier to feel one's way.'

'Are you sure that you can find the way?' asked Polly, beginning again to feel unsure about being led by the strange man.

He squeezed her hand tightly and she knew that she could not have pulled away from him if she had wanted to. 'Don't worry. I'll get you home all right.'

'Do you know if there is a telephone near here?' Polly asked. 'If there is I'd like to telephone my parents.'

'I'm afraid I don't know. But there is no need for that, you'll be home soon.'

They were moving much faster than Polly had managed on her own. She still couldn't see. Even the man beside her was simply a dark shape, but he moved forwards almost as if he could see, pulling Polly with him.

'This is the worst fog I can remember,' said Polly.

'Is it now?' replied the man. 'I remember very bad

fogs when I was a boy, real pea-soupers, but maybe that was before your time. I can't see your face, but you sound young. How old are you?'

'Just twenty,' said Polly.

'Ah twenty! A nice age to be. Watch here, there's a step. We should be at the corner soon.'

'I thought I knew the district well,' said Polly, 'but I'm quite lost tonight. Are you sure that you know the way?' She was beginning to feel frightened again.

There were footsteps coming towards them. 'Someone is coming,' said Polly. 'Shall we ask them where we are, just to be sure?'

Her companion laughed again, that soft little laugh, 'You really mustn't worry young lady. I do know the way!' His hold on her hand tightened again. The footsteps had disappeared. 'They've turned off,' he said.

The grateful helper

The stick sounded against the wall. 'Turn here,' he said. Now Polly could hear voices. A light was shining through the fog from the direction of the voices. Polly looked towards it. It came from an open doorway where two people stood talking. Polly called out to them, 'Are we going the right way for Garden Road?'

'First on the right!' a woman called out.

The man at Polly's side laughed again, 'She's right! Not far to go now.'

Polly began to feel better, and sorry that she had felt unsure of the man beside her. 'I'm sorry if I've taken you out of your way,' she said.

'It's no trouble at all,' he said. 'Here we are, Garden Road.' He stopped at the corner and looked down at her. 'Will you be all right now, or would you like me to come right to your home with you?'

'Thank you so much,' said Polly. 'I'll be fine now thank you. It's just the third house along. You're really very kind. I don't know how I would have managed if you had not come along.' She remembered how afraid she had been feeling a few minutes ago, 'Would you like to come along to my home and rest for a while?'

'It's very nice of you my dear,' said the man, 'but I'll be off. I think there may be many more people lost tonight, and I'd like to help them.'

'Do you mean that you're not going home yourself?' asked Polly. 'That you'll go to find someone else who needs help?'

The man laughed. Now, it seemed a happy friendly laugh. 'Yes, young lady, that is just what I mean to do. You see, a fog as bad as this doesn't happen very often. When it does, it gives me the chance to pay back the help that people give me when the sun is shining. Usually there is too much traffic, and crossing roads is very difficult for me. When I'm standing on the edge of the pavement with this stick of mine, I'm very glad of all the help that people give me. A blind person like me can't get across the road without someone helping him, except in a fog like this.'

2

TIME AND PLACE

A strange sight

I first noticed a change in Tom on the day that I met him in the public library. It is quite easy for me to remember that, because a library was really the wrong place to find him. One would not expect to find a young man like Tom in a place like that on a bright summer day in the middle of the holidays.

If it had been a football field or the beach, then it would have seemed the right place for Tom to be, but to see him carefully looking at history books in the public library was strange.

All this happened a long time ago, but I remember I waited for him to choose the books he wanted before I went over to him. Tom had never liked reading, but he carried three books to the girl at the desk.

'Hello Tom. Getting some books for a friend?' I asked him. I thought he couldn't possibly be borrowing books for himself.

'Oh, hello.' He smiled. 'No, not for a friend, for myself!' He held one of the books so that I could see the name. 'History,' he said. 'Wonderful subject. The only problem is finding time to read all that I'd like to.'

That day I watched him walk away from the library, two books under his arm and the third one open. He moved slowly down the street, reading as he went. It was a strange sight, for in the first place he had always been the sort of young man who is more interested in sports than in learning, and in the second place he had always disliked history. He had often said to me, 'Who wants to learn all those dull old things?'

The unhappy student

It was not until some years after our meeting in the library that Tom explained the change that had come over him. At the time we were sitting in his room at the university where he was studying history.

'It began,' he said, 'in that same library, just a short time before the day that we met there. The day when you were so surprised to find me borrowing books.'

'That was just before your last school examinations, wasn't it? I remember being so surprised when you passed your history examination.'

'I was very surprised, too,' said Tom. 'At the time I was still a bit puzzled by the change in myself. But look here! I'll tell you the whole story if you like, though you must promise not to tell anyone else. People would think I was mad.'

I had a feeling it was going to be a good story. 'I promise,' I said quickly.

'As you know,' Tom began, 'I had always hated history, but at school I had to study it. Well, one day I was told to read some Greek history. I don't mind telling you that when I was given things like that to do I hated my history teacher more than anyone in the world. When I look back I can see that he was really very nice to me, but at the time I could have killed him. The idea of sitting with a dull old history book for hours, trying to remember the names of a lot of dead Greek people — it made me so unhappy.'

I didn't stop Tom talking, but I could have told him just how his old history teacher would have felt.

'No matter how much I hated history, I just had to study it. I had done so badly at school. You see I wasn't really good at anything.

'I decided to make an effort by sitting in the public library where I would not be able to think about other things. I thought that sitting amongst all those books would make it easier for me. I must have sat in that library for more than an hour just looking at nothing, trying to feel right about studying.

'There were not many people there that day and, in the back of my mind, I think I was hoping that someone I knew would come in, then I would talk to them and have an excuse for not working.

'The tables near me were all empty. In fact there was no one in sight when I at last decided to start reading. It didn't really matter very much what I read as long as it was about Greek history. I took the first book that I could find. It was a large dull-looking book called *A History of Greece*.

'Well, I opened it and began to read. There were pictures in the book and after a while I began simply turning the pages, looking at the pictures and reading the words beneath them.

Then, just for a moment I closed my eyes and rested my head in my hands. I'm quite sure that I did not go to sleep, I just closed my eyes. I was tired of trying to think about such a dull subject.

'I only had my eyes closed for a minute or so. I didn't fall asleep.' Tom seemed to be making a lot of this point, so I told him, 'Oh I believe you Tom. Why shouldn't I? So you didn't fall asleep! Please go on.'

An old history teacher

'Well, when I opened my eyes there was an old man sitting there opposite me. I hadn't heard him come in and I must have looked surprised at seeing him there, because he smiled and asked if it was all right for him to sit there. He was silent for a few minutes and then he began to talk. His long thin finger pointed to the book in front of me and he said that it was interesting. Of course I didn't argue with him, even though I didn't really agree. But it soon became clear to me that he knew a lot about Greek history, for he started to tell me things that were in that book as if he'd written it himself. He made it sound as if those long-dead Greeks were part of today's world.

'To tell you the truth I didn't listen to everything he said, but the way in which he said things made it all sound very interesting. Can you understand? It was the way in which he spoke, more than what he said, that was interesting. His way of speaking and the look on his face.

'It was an old face, a very old face, and I found myself thinking about just how old he was. Though the face was lined and the colour of his skin almost grey, the eyes that looked out from under his untidy white hair were young eyes, the eyes of a man who is full of life.

'I think he must have been with me for about half an hour, and he talked about Greek history the whole time. Yet when he was gone the only thing I could remember was the last thing he'd said. He'd said "Time and place are not important. People are important, because the things they did and said make our life what it is today. The time they lived is not important, the place they lived in is not important." The words didn't mean much to me at the time, but for some strange reason I remembered them.

'I watched him walk slowly through the library door, and when he was out of sight I looked down at the book in front of me and began turning the pages looking for more pictures. Then suddenly he was there! Looking up at me from the page. The same untidy white hair, the same shining eyes in the same old lined face. Underneath the picture were the words *Aristotle, 384— 322 BC*. I looked hard at the picture for a long time. There was no mistake — it was the same face.

'Now you know the story. Now you know how my interest in history began. I still cannot really explain it, but since that time I have found all history interesting, though as you know, Greek history is my special interest.'

I didn't quite know what to say to Tom when he had finished his story. I couldn't tell him that he'd been dreaming, he was so sure that he had not fallen asleep. You see, I had been Tom's history teacher during his school days, and the dream, or whatever it was, had succeeded where I had failed.

3

THE LOAN

Life at the bank

Henry Atkins had worked in a small town branch of the Great Eastern Bank for twenty years, and Henry's life was very dull.

He was not a man who looked for excitement in his life. His most exciting dreams were about being sent to a city branch. Working in a city branch would be wonderful, he thought. There would be important people — people who used large sums of money, people who bought and sold great businesses, and he, Henry, would be a part of it.

For twenty years he had received and paid out very small sums of money to the shopkeepers of the town. There were no rich or important people! The richest man in the town was a builder and Henry did not think him very important. He usually came into the bank dressed in his working clothes.

Part of Henry's work was to open the letters which arrived in the morning post.

Letters from the bank's Head Office were always about everyday things, never about anything exciting. Other letters were usually from people asking for loans. Sometimes one of these letters would give Henry a good laugh because of the strange reasons that people gave for needing money.

These were the only times that Henry laughed when he was at work.

This story is really not about Henry Atkins at all, though Henry played a part in it. The story is about someone who didn't even know Henry's name. For even though they met, Henry was just a face behind a desk at the bank.

An important letter

Sir Nathanial Marks was the sort of important man that Henry looked up to. He had started life in a working class home, the son of a tailor. Having learnt his father's business he had started a small factory which made clothes by the use of modern machinery. His business had grown, and by the age of thirty he had over ten factories. Some people said he had more than twenty, but he owned them in different names so that he did not have to pay so much tax. He paid his workers very little money. He stole ideas from other companies. By the age of thirty-five, he had become a millionaire.

At fifty he was one of the richest men in the country. By that time he was buying and selling houses. He had built thousands of cheap homes for working people, all of which were close to the factories in which Nathanial had a business interest.

He enjoyed the money which he made from the cheap homes far more than the workers enjoyed living in them. The men who worked for him, whose job it was to tell the newspapers what to write about him, all said what a kind man he was. So this was noticed by the head of the Government, and he became 'Sir' Nathanial Marks.

And so it was that one morning when Henry Atkins was opening the morning post, he was surprised and excited to see the name 'Sir Nathanial Marks' in a letter from the bank's Head Office. Henry read the letter through three times to make sure that he was not dreaming.

Unlike Henry, the manager of the bank, Alfred Bromley, did not like surprises. Mr Bromley was an average man, with an average wife, and an average family, and he lived in an average house. He was a man who was happiest if nothing new or interesting ever happened. He not only disliked surprises, he disliked changes of any kind.

Henry placed the letters on Mr Bromley's desk. There were only four letters that morning: two asking for loans (and neither of them funny), one giving the date of the town's flower show, and the exciting one from Head Office. Henry placed the exciting one on the top.

Waiting to be called in

Mr Bromley did not look up as Henry entered. Henry did not put the letters down and leave. Instead, he just stood there. Mr Bromley looked up, 'Yes Atkins, was there something?' He always called Henry 'Atkins' when they were in the bank, but if they met in the street he would say 'Good morning, Henry'. It was one of the little rules which Mr Bromley made for himself, little rules that governed his life and helped to keep everything in order.

'The letters, sir, the morning post,' said Henry. He always called Mr Bromley 'sir' in or out of the bank.

He had once made the mistake, when they had met at a party, of calling his manager 'Alfred'. The result of this mistake had been that Mr Bromley had not spoken to him for two days, and had looked very worried whenever they had passed each other. Henry had not made the same mistake again.

'I can see that you've brought the morning post,' said Mr Bromley. 'Was there something else?'

'No sir, nothing else.'

'Well?'

'No sir, nothing sir,' repeated Henry. He left the office feeling disappointed that Mr Bromley had not looked at the exciting letter.

It was, however, only a matter of time before the manager would read the letter. He was a man of habit who did everything in the same order every day. If reading the morning letters was the fourth thing to do, then he would never make it the third.

Henry looked at the clock, it was nine-twenty. He hoped that Mr Bromley would read the letters before lunchtime.

At eleven o'clock the office boy, whose name was John Moreton-Smith, and whom everyone called 'John', took Mr Bromley's coffee in.

As the office boy came out of the manager's office, Henry called him over. 'John,' said Henry, 'did you notice if Mr Bromley had read the morning post?'

'I really couldn't say, Mr Atkins. Would you like me to go in and ask him?' replied John with a cheerful smile.

'No thank you, John. It's not important.'

The door of Mr Bromley's office flew open. Mr Bromley stood in the doorway with a worried look upon his face. 'Ah, Mr Partridge,' he called.

Mr Partridge was the chief clerk. For several years he had also been the acting assistant manager, and he looked forward to the day when he could leave out the word 'acting'. He thought about this every time he saw the words written at the bottom of letters which he had to sign. He disappeared into the manager's office.

'I'll be next,' said Henry, speaking to the money that he was counting. Henry was the 'number three' person in the bank, but this had never given him grand feelings, as below him there was only one clerk, Miss Minter the typist, and the office boy. But being number three man did mean that he could choose what time he would take his holiday each year. It also meant that he was called into Mr Bromley's office when important things were being discussed — things like changes in the times that people went to lunch, for nothing more important ever happened. Today, he felt sure that he would be sent for.

At eleven thirty-five the manager's door re-opened. Mr Partridge appeared. He coughed loudly before

The Loan

27

calling, partly to clear his throat and partly to make sure that everyone looked round before he spoke. 'Ah, Atkins.' Henry, obeying bank rules, locked his money drawer, dropped the keys into his pocket, and went across to the manager's office.

As the door closed upon the three men, the clerk looked at the typist, the typist looked at the office boy, and they all thought, 'What's going on?'

Mr Bromley waited until Mr Partridge and Henry were seated opposite him. In the same way that Mr Partridge had done, he coughed loudly before speaking, 'I have received a letter from Head Office,' he began, 'in which I am told that one of the bank's most important customers will be staying in our town for a short time. As we might all expect, Head Office ask that we give this important person all the help that he may need. I'm sure that both of you know how important this is.

We must make sure that the gentleman knows we are glad to have his business.' He stopped speaking and looked from Mr Partridge to Henry and back again. Looking at them over the top of his glasses, he had the appearance of a school teacher talking to a pair of naughty boys.

Partridge and Henry waited for him to continue.

'The gentleman will arrive this afternoon, and if he should visit us I expect everyone in the bank to be prepared. I understand that he never asks for special attention, but we should make sure that he is given the best attention possible.'

Mr Bromley spoke as if he was making a speech. He always did this when he thought that what he had to say was of great importance.

'The gentleman's name is,' he looked up at his listeners, 'Sir Nathanial Marks.'

Henry looked pleased. Mr Partridge did his best to do the same.

'If you should have to attend to him, Atkins, you are to give him anything he wants, without question. We do not need to follow the usual rules about checking a customer's identity. Not for Sir Nathanial Marks.'

A real millionaire

Mr Bromley dismissed the two men from his office, and a minute later came out of the office himself. He looked around the bank checking that everything was in its correct place, and then went back into his office again.

John, the office boy, whispered to Miss Minter, the typist, 'What's happening?'

'I've no idea, but I'll find out,' she replied. From where Miss Minter sat it was easy to catch the eye of anyone working at the front of the bank. She looked hard at Henry until he looked round, then she smiled at him. It was a smile which she usually kept for the young men who looked at her as she walked down the street. At heart, Henry was a young man. He walked over to where she sat. 'What's happening, Mr Atkins?' she asked, her special smile still in place.

Henry was dying to tell someone. He told Miss Minter. In ten minutes the clerk knew, and John the office boy had also been told. By the time the workers of the Great Eastern Bank had been out for lunch, half the people in the town had been told.

Henry was excited. He would soon meet a real millionaire, a man who lived in the world of big business that Henry dreamed about.

Mr Bromley did not feel happy. He wanted to please the people at Head Office, and he knew the importance of customers like Sir Nathanial Marks. But he wished that they would leave his peaceful well-ordered life to continue in the way that he liked it.

At five minutes to three a big, shiny Rolls Royce drew up outside the Great Eastern Bank.

Remembering what Mr Bromley had said about Sir Nathanial not asking for special attention, Henry stopped himself from rushing out to open the door. Instead, he stood by his desk trying to look busy. In fact he had no work to do at the time.

Mr Partridge tried to look calm, as if such important people were a part of his everyday life.

Miss Minter combed her hair and looked in a small hand-mirror to make sure that her make-up was in order. The clerk went out to the wash-room. He did not want to have to speak to the great man.

'He's coming!' said John, loudly.

Mr Bromley wished he'd taken the day off work.

The millionaire walked into the bank and stood in front

of Henry. 'Good afternoon. My name is Marks, and I ...'

'Good afternoon, sir,' said Henry, not waiting for him to finish. 'We were expecting you, sir. A letter from Head Office advised us that you were coming, sir. May I say, sir ...' Henry had been practising this speech since lunchtime, but he was not allowed to continue.

Sir Nathanial looked amused, 'Yes, yes, quite so. Now, as you already know who I am, I'll come straight to the point. I don't know if you're the right person to ask, but I want to borrow a hundred pounds. Will you lend it to me?'

No need to borrow money

Henry's mouth fell open. Then he laughed, 'Very good, sir! Yes, a very good joke, sir! Oh very funny, sir!'

At the sound of Henry's laughter, both John and Miss Minter smiled broadly as if they shared the joke, though they could not possibly have heard what was said. At the same time Mr Partridge looked very serious. He did not think it right to laugh in front of important customers. In his office, Mr Bromley said a prayer.

'My good man,' said the millionaire, who had not even smiled when Henry laughed, 'I am not in the habit of making jokes about money.'

'Oh!' The smile disappeared from Henry's face. 'But you said that you wanted to borrow a hundred pounds.'

'Exactly! All I want to know is, will you lend me a hundred pounds? Now! Will you lend it to me or not?'

'Oh dear,' thought Henry, 'this is not at all what I expected.' He did not want to call Mr Partridge for advice. To do so would throw away his big chance to talk to someone really important. Mr Partridge, who had heard part of what had been said, was hoping that Henry would not call him.

Taking a deep breath Henry tried to put his point as politely as possible. 'Sir, you have no need to borrow money. The bank will be quite happy to take your cheque for whatever amount you need.'

It was Nathanial Marks's turn to take a deep breath. He spoke slowly as if he was talking to a simple-minded child, 'I am quite sure that you're right! I'm sure that the bank will take my cheque. I do not need you to tell me that, for I do have some little knowledge in matters of money. I would, on the other hand be pleased if you would agree to LEND ME A HUNDRED POUNDS.' He shouted the last words so loudly that everyone in the bank heard him. He looked around him, then back at Henry, and whispered, 'Without telling anyone about it.'

'Sir, I ...' Henry began to speak, to try again to make the great man understand what he meant, then changed his mind. 'If you would not mind waiting a few seconds sir, I'll call the manager.' Without waiting for a reply, Henry left Sir Nathanial and crossed to Mr Bromley's office.

Keeping the customer happy

Hearing Henry's knock, Mr Bromley stopped praying. 'Oh no!' he said aloud, and, lifting his eyes to heaven, he added, 'Not problems, please!' Then in a louder voice, 'Come in.'

Henry explained, at least he thought that he explained, but even as he was doing so the words sounded foolish. 'Nonsense, nonsense, nonsense!' said Mr Bromley, pushing Henry out of the way. Fixing a smile on his face, he went out of the office towards the waiting millionaire. 'Sir Nathanial,' he said, an outstretched hand held towards the great man. 'They didn't tell me you were here, do come through, please.'

Nathanial Marks did not reply, but walked straight past the outstretched hand, and into the office. Mr Bromley skipped along behind him like a little boat dancing on the sea behind a big ship.

It was not that Marks was so big, nor that Bromley was so small. It was the way that they behaved that made the whole thing look so funny. Miss Minter, Mr Partridge, John and the clerk all laughed quietly to themselves as the pair went by. There had never been laughter in the Great Eastern Bank. The place would never be the same again.

Seated behind his desk Mr Bromley felt just a little better. His office was a place of safety, which is why he didn't often leave it. 'Ah now, Sir Nathanial,' he began. 'We heard you were coming. A letter advising us arrived this morning. May I say how very pleased we are to have you call upon our little branch, and ...'

'I heard all that from the man outside.' Sir Nathanial Marks was not famous for being either polite or patient. 'Can we get down to business?'

'Ah yes, quite so!' In his mind Mr Bromley hated Henry for having said it before him, forgetting that he had left it all to Henry in the first place.

'My man had some silly idea that you wanted to borrow money.'

'I do! A hundred pounds!'

'But ...' Mr Bromley was stuck for words. His eyes were again lifted to heaven. 'Help!' he said quietly. 'Sir Nathanial, you are a very rich man; you do not need to borrow money. I am sure that you know that the bank would be most happy to change a cheque for you, and I ...'

'I heard all that as well, from the man outside. I'm beginning to ask myself if you are all deaf in this branch. I've asked a simple question: will you, or will you not lend me a hundred pounds? All you need to do is to answer yes or no.'

Mr Bromley was silent. 'The old boy is mad,' he thought, 'quite mad! That's the only possible explanation.'

'Well?' said Sir Nathanial. 'What's it to be, yes or no?'

'I'd better keep him happy,' thought Mr Bromley. He remembered the letter from Head Office. It had said that they should give Marks anything he wanted. Maybe they knew he was mad. He smiled a gentle smile and said 'Yes, Sir Nathanial, yes of course we'll lend you a hundred pounds.'

'Right! Thank heavens that's decided. Let me have a hundred pounds in ten-pound notes and I'll sign for it.' Mr Bromley went to the safe, carefully counted out ten ten-pound notes and put them on the desk in front of his visitor.

'You must never be sure of anyone'

Marks gathered the money from the desk and pushed it carelessly into his pocket. 'Right! Let's have your forms or whatever it is that customers have to sign.'

'Oh that will not be necessary Sir Nathanial. Not necessary at all. There is no need for that sort of thing.' He felt sure that Head Office would simply take the money from the old man's great fortune, and pass it back to his branch.

'Rubbish!' shouted the millionaire, 'of course I have to sign for it. What sort of businessman are you, Mr Bumley?'

'Bromley!' corrected Mr Bromley.

'Come along man, get your forms out and let me sign them.'

By now poor Mr Bromley was so unhappy that he did not know the right thing to do. If only he could have made a telephone call to Head Office for advice, but there had been no time. And even if he had called, the people at Head Office would have thought him foolish for not being able to decide what to do. 'Oh dear, oh dear,' he thought, 'this is like a bad dream.'

He laid the forms in front of Sir Nathanial Marks, 'Sign here,' he said, 'and here. I'll fill in all the other things later, there is no need to trouble you to do that.' He held his breath, hoping that this would be all right.

As he signed the forms Sir Nathanial Marks had a little smile on his face, but Mr Bromley was too unhappy to notice.

'There you are, Mr Bumley,' said Nathanial Marks. 'All signed. Business is business, we must do things properly. Now! What can I offer you, just in case I don't come back to pay you.' He laughed, 'One of the first rules of lending money, Mr Bumley, always make sure that the loan is safe.'

Mr Bromley allowed himself to laugh — he thought it would be in order. 'I'm sure that's not necessary Sir Nathanial,' he said, 'with a tiny sum like a hundred pounds, the bank can be quite sure of a man of your great fortune.' He laughed again. The look on Sir Nathanial's face told him that the laughter was not in order.

'In business, Mr Bumley, you should never be sure of anyone. Such feelings are not a part of business.' He put his hand in his pocket and took out a bunch of keys. 'Here are the keys to my car.' He threw them on the desk. 'Keep the car until I return your hundred pounds.' He stood up and moved towards the door.

Sir Nathaniel's car

Mr Bromley tried to say no, but Sir Nathanial Marks was not listening, he was already halfway out of the office. Mr Bromley was sure that Head Office would not like the idea of his keeping a Rolls Royce for a loan of only a hundred pounds. He was sure that they would not like the way in which he had handled the whole business. 'But,' he told himself, 'what else could I do?'

He was still trying to say no when Sir Nathanial Marks had walked out of the bank and, without even looking at his car, had walked off down the street.

Mr Bromley decided two things. First, he would behave as if nothing strange had happened. Second, he would not tell Head Office anything about it. He turned from the door sadly, the car keys still in his hand. He must not let the others in the bank know what had happened, he thought to himself. Everything must appear as if he, Alfred Bromley, had decided things.

'Ah, Atkins! One minute please.'

Henry flew towards the manager's office without stopping to lock his money drawer. 'Yes, sir. Did everything work out all right sir?'

Mr Bromley put a serious look on his face, 'My business with Sir Nathanial was quite successful, Atkins. Nothing for you to think about. Now here are the keys to Sir Nathanial's car. Drive the car round to the yard at the back of the bank, and lock it safely in the garage there, then return the keys to me.'

The bank building had only one garage. This should have been for the manager's car, but as Mr Bromley did not drive, it was empty. Henry drove the car round the block. It only took five minutes, but during that five minutes, he imagined that he was the millionaire owner of the car, on his way to an important business meeting. It was probably the happiest five minutes of Henry's life.

During the next few days, the whole adventure seemed like a dream. It might well have been a dream had it not been for the car. To Henry it had been a grand adventure, and he made sure that it had not been a dream by going to look at the car every lunchtime.

A week went by, then two weeks. Sir Nathanial Marks had not returned. Mr Bromley had had no word from Head Office on the matter. Sometimes he managed to forget the whole thing, sometimes it worried him. Once he had gone to look into the garage, hoping the car would not be there, that the whole thing would turn out to be a dream. He would gladly have paid the hundred pounds from his own pocket if it meant that he did not have to think about it again.

Paying for the loan

It was in fact exactly one month later when, without anyone expecting him, Sir Nathanial Marks appeared in front of Henry.

'Before you begin to tell me how pleased you are to see me,' he said, 'I'd like to see Mr Bumley.'

'Mr Bromley?' said Henry. 'Yes sir. This way please, sir.'

As the door opened to admit Sir Nathanial Marks, Mr Bromley was thinking about how to show the hundred pound loan in his end-of-the-month report to Head Office. He had almost decided not to show it at all; this would have been quite dishonest, but so much easier than trying to make explanations. Mr Bromley hated writing long reports.

Mr Bromley jumped to his feet. Sir Nathanial sat down, and his hand went to his pocket. He placed ten ten-pound notes on the desk. Mr Bromley felt sure that they were the same ones that he'd taken from the safe a month ago.

'There's your hundred,' said Sir Nathanial smiling. 'How much do I have to pay for the loan?'

Mr Bromley felt better already. He could now tear up the loan forms and say nothing about it; nobody would know about it. 'I'm sure that we don't have to worry about such a small sum Sir Nathanial. Forget about it!' He was smiling cheerfully.

'My dear Mr Bumley,' said Sir Nathanial, 'when will you learn?' (Mr Bromley's smile disappeared.) 'Business is business! I'm sure that your head office would not like you to lend people money without earning anything on it.'

'Oh dear,' thought Mr Bromley. 'The old man is quite mad, all I can do is to agree with him.' Aloud, he said, 'Of course not. You're quite right. Quite so, quite so! I'll just work it out. He pulled a sheet of paper towards him and began writing, speaking softly to himself as he did so, 'One hundred pounds for one month at …'

He looked up. Sir Nathanial Marks was smiling broadly. 'It's exactly forty-two pence.'

'Right! Forty-two pence it is.' Sir Nathanial placed the coins on the desk and got to his feet. 'Now if you would kindly let me have my car.'

The business agreement

Mr Bromley was only too pleased to say goodbye to Sir Nathanial Marks, and his car. He opened the office door, 'Ah, Atkins.'

Henry rushed forward, smiling through the open door at the great man. 'He may be a little mad,' thought Henry, 'but he's still an important customer.'

'Atkins, bring Sir Nathanial's car round to the front, will you?' He handed Henry the keys. A little sadly, Henry drove the beautiful shiny Rolls Royce to the front of the bank. Mr Bromley and Sir Nathanial were waiting at the front door. Obeying a look from Mr Bromley, Henry went through the door and back to his dull life behind his dull desk.

Seated behind the driving wheel, Sir Nathanial lowered the window. 'Well Bumley, do you want to know why?' There was a broad smile on the millionaire's face. Mr Bromley was not sure that he did want to know why about anything. He was just pleased that Sir Nathanial was going out of his life (for ever, he hoped). He would be pleased to get back to his safe little world where nothing ever happened.

'It was a bet you see, Bumley. I bet a man at my club ten thousand pounds that I could make a good business agreement that would allow me to garage a Rolls Royce for less than fifty pence a month. The fool said I couldn't do it without asking for a special favour. But I did it, didn't I Bumley? You were not doing me a favour, were you? It was a business agreement.'

4
THE TRUTH

Miss Marchant's ideas

'The truth,' said Miss Marchant, 'is beautiful.' She looked at the young faces before her. A few faces showed interest, but most of them showed that Miss Marchant was not getting their attention.

This made Miss Marchant feel sad. Her efforts in twenty-five years of teaching had not been very successful, but she had never given up trying. Those people who worked with her, and those who had done so in the past, all knew that Miss Marchant was the sort of person who had a strong belief in the things she taught.

Though she had never given up trying, there were times when she found it difficult to go on. This afternoon, she felt, was one of those times.

To put into the mind of a child an understanding of the truth was a job which she considered important, but one in which she had never been completely successful. She thought that her failures were not the result of poor ability, but the result of the way in which everything in life seemed to work against her.

She thought about the notes which children brought to school. They were usually badly written notes on untidy pieces of paper which were signed by the parents of her pupils. A note explaining the absence from class of one of her pupils nearly always contained lies. 'Everyone,' she would say, 'tells lies, and children copy them. The world in which they grow up demands that they do not tell the truth.' Then she would make a long speech about the things that were wrong with the modern world, blaming all these bad things on people's failure to tell the truth.

Once Miss Marchant began this speech it was impossible to stop her. Even people who did not know her very well knew about her ideas on the importance of telling the truth.

She was glad when she heard the school bell ring, sounding the end of the last lesson of the day. She gathered the books from her desk, dropped them into her bag, and made her way to the teachers' room.

The letter

Home, to Miss Marchant, was a neat little three-bedroom flat which she shared with her potted plants and a great number of photographs of aunts, uncles, nieces, nephews and cousins. She had lived there almost all of her working life. As she opened the front door, she noticed a letter lying waiting for her. Stepping over it, she first entered the sitting-room where she put down her bag. Then, crossing to the bedroom she took off her street clothes, and it was not until she had made a cup of tea that she looked at the letter.

She did not receive many letters. The relatives who looked down at her from the walls did not write to her. They may have forgotten her completely, and the only reason that she remembered them was their photographs.

She certainly did not know the writing on the envelope. Opening the letter, she put on her glasses and began to read: '... I have been told about your ability as a teacher and I would like you to give lessons to my eight-year-old son. He needs to have lessons at home because there is some difficulty in sending him to school. You could give the lessons at any time that would be best for you ...' The letter was signed 'Mary Sharpe'.

The address from which the letter had been sent was only a short walking distance from Miss Marchant's flat. She liked the sound of the letter, it was direct and to the point, as if the writer was an honest person. She wanted to know why young Master Sharpe needed lessons at home, and why it was difficult to send him to school. Looking at the clock, she decided to go and find out immediately.

The disadvantage

Standing at the front door of Mrs Sharpe's house half an hour later, Miss Marchant was pleased to see some potted plants in the window of the front room. 'We both like plants,' she said to herself. She began to feel sure that she would like Mrs Sharpe.

Mrs Mary Sharpe opened the front door. She was a neatly dressed lady in her mid-thirties who was as direct in her speech as she had been in her letter.

'I'm glad you came so quickly Miss Marchant. If you agree to teach young Nicholas I will be so pleased. I don't feel that I'm able to do the job myself.'

'First,' said Miss Marchant, 'I would like to know why your son needs to have lessons at home.'

'The problem,' said Mrs Sharpe, 'is that when Nicholas goes to school he has a disadvantage which makes it impossible for him to learn anything.'

'A disadvantage! What sort of disadvantage?'

'His trouble is,' Mrs Sharpe stopped as if she was not sure that she should say what was in her mind, then, taking a deep breath, 'he always tells the truth.'

A smile of joy spread over Miss Marchant's face, 'But that's wonderful! I can't think why you call that a disadvantage. The truth is something I feel very strongly about. That's really wonderful!'

The smile on Mrs Sharpe's face was not one of joy, but she was clearly amused by Miss Marchant's words.

'Believe me, Miss Marchant, telling the truth is a great disadvantage. My husband and I have tried to stop Nicholas from doing it, but so far we have not succeeded. He always tells the truth, the whole truth, and nothing but the truth.'

Truthful answers

Miss Marchant did not know what to say. All her life she had been saying that the answer to all the world's problems was to be found in simply telling the truth. For twenty-five years she had been trying to help her pupils understand this. Now she was about to meet a boy who did so without any help, and she was puzzled by his parents' strange ideas.

'The truth,' she said, a religious note in her voice, 'is beautiful.'

'Not always, Miss Marchant. In fact, not very often,' said Mrs Sharpe a little sadly.

'Where is the young man? I'd like to meet him.'

'He's playing in the garden. Before I call him, may I ask if the job interests you? We can talk about times and money later on, but I'd like to know if you'll take the job.'

Miss Marchant never did understand why she did not decide immediately. Normally she was quick to make up her mind, but now something held her back, and she was not sure what. It was just a feeling. 'I'd like to meet Nicholas first,' she said.

Mrs Sharpe looked out across the large garden. At the far corner Miss Marchant could see a small fair-haired boy playing on the grass. Mrs Sharpe opened the window. 'Nicholas,' she called. 'Would you like to come in for a minute?'

The boy lifted his head. Holding his hands around his mouth Nicholas shouted back, 'No, thank you!'

'Oh dear,' said Mrs Sharpe. 'I'm sorry about that. I always forget that if I ask a question he'll simply answer it, truthfully of course.'

Miss Marchant was not sure that she understood. Seeing the puzzled look on her face, Mrs Sharpe explained, 'I asked him if he'd like to come in, and he answered truthfully that he wouldn't like to.' She turned again to the window, 'Nicholas, please come in for a minute.' As if he had been expecting this, the boy started towards the house.

Nicholas Sharpe was a good-looking boy. He was eight years old. He stood in front of Miss Marchant, his serious blue eyes fixed on hers.

'Hello Nicholas,' said Miss Marchant, feeling strangely uncomfortable. 'I'm sorry if I stopped your game in the garden. What were you playing?'

'Yes, I'm sorry too,' replied the boy. 'I wasn't playing, I was building something.'

'And what were you building?'

Nicholas's eyes were still fixed on Miss Marchant's face. 'I'd rather not explain. It would take too long and I don't think that you would understand.'

'Oh!' Miss Marchant was not sure what to say next.

'Nicholas! That was not polite!' said Mrs Sharpe. 'Miss Marchant showed an interest in what you were doing and you were rude to her.' She held the boy's arm, turning him again to face their visitor. 'Say that you're sorry to Miss Marchant.'

'But I'm not sorry,' said Nicholas. 'Old ladies never do understand what I do, and it's a waste of time trying to explain to them.'

A change in Miss Marchant

Mrs Sharpe looked angry. She did not like her son saying that Miss Marchant was old, but Miss Marchant laughed even though she was not amused. 'I'm sure that Nicholas is right Mrs Sharpe. I probably wouldn't understand. I'm sure that Nicholas would find it a waste of time trying to explain to me.'

The serious look on the boy's face did not change. 'You're right,' he said, 'I would. And I don't think you're really interested in what I was doing. You only asked me because you wanted to be polite.'

For a minute there was silence in the room, then Nicholas said, 'Are you the teacher that Mummy wrote to?'

This was the sort of thing that Miss Marchant was used to hearing from little boys. She smiled brightly:

'Yes, that's right, dear.'

Her smile quickly disappeared as Nicholas said, 'I'd like to know about your strange ideas.'

Both Mrs Sharpe and Miss Marchant spoke at the same time.

'Nicholas, really!'

'My what, dear?'

Taking no notice of his mother's words, Nicholas answered Miss Marchant's question. 'I heard Mummy's friend tell her that you were a funny old bird who had some strange ideas, but that you were a good teacher. I can see that you look funny, and now I'd like to know about your strange ideas.'

It was only about a week after Miss Marchant's meeting with Master Nicholas Sharpe that the other teachers at the school where she worked began to notice a change in her. 'Do you think she's ill?' asked one. 'She hasn't given anyone her advice on telling the truth for days now. There must be something wrong with her.'

'It's possible,' said another, 'that someone has been brave enough to tell her the truth.'

5
TAXI

Waiting for a passenger

Ken sat behind the wheel of his taxi, which was parked at the side of the road. His eyes were closed and his thoughts were not on his work. He was not asleep, and he was not dreaming, but the warm sun that fell on him through the window was turning his thoughts away from work — to more pleasant things.

His last passenger had been a young man, younger than Ken. A well-dressed young man who had carried a very good quality bag. Ken had taken him to the Plaza Hotel. The man had run quickly up the steps to the entrance. The doorman had opened the door for him very politely.

'He's an important businessman,' thought Ken. 'Possibly on his way to an important meeting. He will probably have lunch with other businessmen after the meeting, a wonderful lunch with nice things to drink.'

Ken's thoughts took him one by one through each of the dishes that he imagined that the man might have. Then he thought of the simple food that he himself would eat later.

Ken's first passengers that morning had been a man and his wife on their way to the airport. 'Hurry driver!' they had told him. 'If we miss the eight o'clock plane to New York we'll not arrive in time for the plane to San Francisco.'

They had five large bags which Ken had helped to carry into the airport building. Ken thought of the clothes at home in his bedroom. They would all have fitted into one of those bags.

The woman had been very
beautiful, and dressed in beautiful
clothes. Ken thought of his wife — she was beautiful
but her clothes always looked old. She never asked for
beautiful things, but Ken wished very much that he
could buy some for her.

He thought of people flying half way round the
world, people living in grand hotels, wearing beautiful
clothes, eating the best food. Ken had been born in the
town where he worked, and he'd never been out of it.
'I'll probably die here as well,' he thought. 'I'll go on
working, driving this taxi for twelve hours a day, then
I'll die here.'

The foreigner

He was deep in thought when there was a knock on
the window. It made him jump! He opened his
eyes, and leaned across to open the back door. The
passenger was a tall, thin man, about fifty years old. He
threw a small bag on to the seat, and got in.

Ken put on a smile, his polite taxi-driver's smile. 'Good morning, sir. Where to?'

Without replying, the man handed Ken a piece of paper with an address written on it. 'A foreigner,' thought Ken, 'he doesn't speak English.' Ken looked at the paper. The address was that of a house in a very rich neighbourhood. 'Yes, sir,' Ken handed the paper back to the passenger.

As the taxi moved through the busy streets Ken began to think about his passenger. In the mirror he studied the man's face. 'Not the usual businessman,' he thought, 'but a stranger, or he would have spoken the address instead of having it written down. Maybe a foreigner who is here to see friends.'

After ten years of driving a taxi, Ken had a very good knowledge of people. He was able to look at most people and guess what work they did. The passenger who now sat behind him was a difficult one to decide upon. When Ken looked in the mirror again he could not see the man's face, for he was holding up a newspaper. Ken read the headlines at the top of the front page: 'POLICE QUESTION MAN WHO SAW BANK ROBBERY'.

Ken did not have time to read the newspaper in the mornings. He usually did so after arriving home in the evenings. In yesterday's newspaper there had been a report about a bank robbery. The thieves had stolen more than five hundred thousand dollars. 'By now,' thought Ken, 'they will be flying around the world like the two people I took to the airport this morning.'

The taxi was now speeding through a part of the town where there was less traffic, where big houses stood far from the road, each one in its own beautiful garden. Turning into the gate of one of the houses, Ken drove up the steep slope that led to the front door.

As the taxi stopped, the man in the back leant forward, pushed some money into Ken's hand, and opened the door. He moved quickly from the taxi to the front door of the house which was opened for him before he reached it. 'He was expected,' thought Ken. It seemed that someone inside the house had been ready to receive him, and had heard the taxi coming.

Police check

Ken drove slowly back towards the centre of the town, hoping for another passenger. He did not get one until he was nearly into the busy part. The passenger was a man Ken knew by sight.

'How's business?' the man asked.

'The same as usual,' answered Ken. 'Every day is the same. The only thing that changes is the faces of my passengers.'

The man got out of the taxi in the centre of the town and Ken drove slowly towards the nearest hotel. Hotels were good places to find passengers, and he was in luck! The doorman of the hotel was waving to him. Ken drove the taxi to the side of the road and stopped in front of the hotel.

The doorman started to put bags into the back of the taxi. He opened the door as two men appeared on the hotel steps. One of them handed some money to the doorman who touched his cap in thanks and said to Ken, 'The airport, driver.'

Ken thought that this was very bad luck. Once out at the airport, which was several miles from the town, he might have a long wait before getting a passenger back to town. There were always a lot of taxis waiting there, and he would have to take his turn. That morning he had waited nearly an hour before a passenger came.

On the drive out to the airport the two men in the back kept talking about business matters. Ken could only understand a little of what they said. Business matters were something that he had no knowledge of.

As they turned into the road that led to the airport, Ken noticed several policemen standing there. Fifty yards further on a police sign on the side of the road said 'SLOW — POLICE CHECK'. 'Another thing to waste my time,' thought Ken.

The two men in the back stopped talking. They had also seen the sign.

'What's going on, driver?' asked one.

'Police check, sir,' said Ken. 'I expect they are looking for the men who robbed the bank yesterday.'

'Well I hope it won't take long; we have a plane to catch.'

'In this morning's paper,' said the second man, 'it said that somebody saw the whole thing. He heard one of the robbers talking and said he sounded like a foreigner.'

'Yes, I read that. It seems that one of the thieves dropped a handkerchief in the bank, but I can't see that that will help the police. It's hard trying to find someone by looking at his handkerchief.' Both men laughed loudly.

'We've got something here'

As Ken stopped the taxi, two policemen came towards them. There must have been twenty or more policemen there. Some were looking at other cars. Some were talking to the drivers.

One policeman stood with a big dog beside him. It was beside the car in front of Ken's.

Ken got out of the taxi as the two policemen reached it. 'Just checking, driver,' said one.

'Well, I haven't got five hundred thousand dollars hidden under the seat,' said Ken.

'Well, we'll have to see about that, won't we?' said the policeman without even smiling. He walked around the taxi looking at it with care.

The second policeman spoke to the passengers. 'Can I see your plane tickets please, gentlemen?'

Ken smiled to himself, 'They're "gentlemen",' he thought. 'I'm just "driver".' The first policeman was now opening the back of the taxi. 'Don't ask!' thought Ken. 'Just help yourself. Don't say please! I'm only the driver.'

The policeman holding the dog was coming towards them. He stopped at the front of the taxi and took from his pocket a small bag. Ken could see that the bag contained a small white cloth — a handkerchief!

The policeman opened the bag and held it to the dog's nose then, bending over, he spoke softly to the dog.

Slowly he started to circle the car. The dog was smelling the sides of the taxi. Suddenly, when it reached the passenger door, it became very excited.

'I think we've got something here, sir,' the policeman shouted out.

At once, policemen were moving towards Ken's taxi. One of them opened the back door. 'Would you get out.' It was not a question, but an order.

'Oh!' thought Ken. 'They aren't gentlemen any more, and he didn't say "please".'

The two men got out, looking very annoyed, 'Look here, officer, we have a plane to catch! What's all this about, anyway?'

'If you would just stand away from the taxi for a minute,' said the policeman, without answering the question.

The handkerchief

The policeman with the dog led it a few yards away from Ken's taxi and again took the bag from his pocket and held it to the dog's nose. Immediately the dog pulled towards the taxi and, taking no notice of the passengers who now stood on the pavement, it went straight to the open door and jumped inside.

Ken stood watching the dog. He was beginning to understand what was happening. If the dog had picked up the smell of the handkerchief in his car, and the handkerchief had belonged to one of the robbers, then ...

His thoughts on the matter were not allowed to continue. A policeman in plain clothes spoke to him, 'I'm Inspector West. I'd like you to come along to the police station to answer a few questions.'

'But what about my passengers?' asked Ken. 'And I have work to do. I have my living to earn.'

'We'll take care of your passengers and we'll try not to keep you any longer than necessary.'

Policemen were already taking the bags from the taxi and putting them into one of the police cars. 'If you're ready, sir, we can get started,' said the inspector. As he spoke, he got into Ken's taxi and sat beside the driver's seat.

As they drove away, Ken thought, 'He called me "sir".'

At the police station

Half an hour later, seated in the inspector's office at the police station, Ken was trying to remember all the passengers that he had had that day.

'Now think again, sir,' said Inspector West. 'Your first passengers were a man and a woman. You took them to the airport. That was before our people knew that the handkerchief belonged to one of the robbers, and therefore before we had set up the road block. You say that the man was young and tall, and that the woman was beautiful and well-dressed. What else can you remember about them?'

'I've had a lot of passengers since then,' said Ken. 'It's very difficult to remember the first ones.' Ken had always thought that he had a good memory, but now he was not so sure. 'I've told you all I can. I can't think why you people didn't set up your check on the airport straight after the robbery.'

'Yes I can understand your surprise,' said the Inspector. 'People think that we can just stop everybody at the airport and examine their bags, but it's not as simple as that. We have to get permission from the people at the top, and sometimes that is very difficult. We don't like to delay thousands of people if we are not sure. But when we had the handkerchief we knew that with that, and a good police dog, we could get permission to stop people at the airport. Now all we have to do is to call on all the people who have been in your taxi since the robbery.'

'Well as I've told you, the taxi was cleaned out completely last night, and washed and polished.'

'Which means,' said the Inspector, 'that somebody who handled the handkerchief has been in it today.' Again Ken told the Inspector all he could remember about the day's passengers.

When Ken had finished, the inspector sat thinking. Ken waited patiently.

At last the inspector looked up, 'All right, sir, you are free to go now. My men have checked the back seat of your taxi for finger-prints, but I do not think that it will do us any good. If they find the finger-prints of anyone who is known to us, then I'll be very surprised.'

Ken stood up, 'Well I'm glad that that is over. I can get back to work. I've lost enough time already.'

Inspector West walked to the door with him. 'By the way, sir,' he said, 'if anyone should get in touch with you over this, anyone other than our people, please telephone me.'

Something is wrong

It was not until he was driving away from the police station that Ken thought about the inspector's words. 'Who would get in touch with me, other than the police?' he thought. Then dismissing the thought from his mind, he drove slowly along the road, his eyes open for passengers.

Arriving home that night, Ken climbed the stairs to the third floor flat where he lived with his wife, Mabel. He was asking himself whether or not he should tell Mabel about what had happened. Mabel was a clever girl, but she might get frightened. She read the newspaper every day, and often talked about the terrible things that happened. Ken did not want to frighten his wife, and if he told her about the robbery, the police, and that the robbers had been in his taxi, she might imagine all sorts of terrible things.

He put the key in the lock and turned it. As he did so he had a feeling that something was wrong.

The first thing he saw as he pushed open the door was unusual. Mabel was sitting in the big chair facing him, and the unusual thing about this was that Mabel never used that chair. She didn't like it. Another unusual thing was that the chair was never in that place, facing the door.

Closing the door behind him he began, 'What's wrong?' Mabel, without turning her head, was looking to her left. Ken, following the direction of her eyes, turned his head and found himself facing a man holding a gun. The gun was pointing straight at Mabel.

Like most people, Ken had often thought about what he would do if this sort of thing happened. He had been sure that he would be too frightened to do anything. Strangely, he now felt quite calm.

'Who's this?'

The man with the gun pointed to the chair next to Mabel's, 'Sit down!'

'Now you look here ...!' Ken began again.

The gun turned and pointed straight at Ken's head. The man spoke slowly, 'I said sit down!'

Ken sat down, his eyes fixed on the man's face.

Ken understands

The man behind the gun was, Ken judged, in his mid-thirties. His face showed no feelings, but the eyes were cruel and hard. He looked as if he would be quick to use the gun if he was not obeyed. His voice, however, was soft, the voice of an educated man.

Without letting his eyes move from Ken's face, the man sat down facing Ken and Mabel. Ken took hold of Mabel's hand comfortingly.

A smile appeared on the visitor's face as he spoke, but it was not a pleasant smile, 'You have a very pretty wife, Mr taxi driver. It would be terrible if anything happened to her.'

Ken moved as if to get up. The man stopped smiling. 'Sit.' Ken sat back in his chair, and the man smiled again. 'That's better! Now nothing will happen to her, or to you, if …', Ken could hear the sound of the man's heavy breathing, '… if you do as you are told.'

'If you didn't have that gun, I'd …' Ken began.

'Ah! But I do have the gun, Mr taxi driver.' The voice was hard. 'So you had better keep quiet and listen to me.' If it had not been for Mabel, Ken would have attacked the man, gun or no gun.

'Tomorrow,' said the man, 'the police will telephone you. They will ask you to go down to the police station to help them. They will line up a number of people and ask you to pick out anyone that you have seen before. Amongst those people will be some of the passengers that you have had today. If you are wise, you will tell them that you have never seen any of the people before.' The gun moved up and down like a finger being waved under the nose of a naughty child. 'Do you understand, Mr taxi driver?'

Ken understood well enough. The police had caught one of the bank robbers, one who had been in his taxi. They would want Ken to pick him out. If he did so then this man, who was probably another of the robbers, would do something to Mabel.

An important message

The man stood up and moved towards the door, 'I'm going now, but I will not be far away. I like the look of your pretty wife. It would be sad if …'

As the door closed Mabel burst into tears. 'Ken, Ken! What's happened? What is this all about? I don't understand!'

Ken's arms were round her, she was shaking with fear. He kissed the tears from her eyes. 'There, there, my love. It's all right, nothing is going to happen,' he said. 'You mustn't worry, there's no need to be frightened.'

Though he tried to comfort Mabel and to sound calm, Ken was thinking hard. There had to be a way to beat these people.

He told Mabel about the police check, the dog that had smelled something in his car, and his visit to the office of Inspector West.

Finishing the story, he said, 'So that is what the Inspector meant! He said if anyone got in touch with me I should let him know. He must have guessed that this would happen.'

Mabel dried her eyes, 'Ken, if the Inspector knew that they might come here, don't you think that we should tell him?'

Ken smiled at his wife. She had been badly frightened, but she was very brave. His mind was made up. 'You're right! These people can only succeed if we are frightened of them. No one is going to point a gun at me and tell me what to do. I won't let them get away with it.'

Picking up the telephone, Ken called the number which Inspector West had given him. The person at the other end asked who was speaking. Ken thought that it was no good taking chances, 'I don't want to give my name, I only want to speak to Inspector West.'

'I'm sorry but Inspector West has left the office.'

'Well give me his home number.'

'I'm sorry, but I'm not allowed to do that. If you'll tell me what it's about maybe I can help you.'

'Can you get in touch with Inspector West?'

There was a short silence, then, 'Yes, I could.'

'Well, you call him and tell him to take good care of his dog. He'll understand.'

'His dog?'

'Yes! He'll understand.'

The voice at the other end sounded puzzled, 'All right, I'll pass your message on.'

'And please do so now,' said Ken. 'It's important.'

'What was all that about?' asked Mabel. 'Why didn't you tell them about the man?'

Ken took her face gently in his hands, 'Listen, Mabel, I don't want to take any chances. I believe that Inspector West is a good man. There was something about him that made me feel sure I could believe in him. I don't want anyone else to know what I'm going to tell him, just in case the bank robbers hear about it.'

'To thank you for your help'

Ten minutes later the telephone rang. Ken and Mabel were both in the kitchen. 'A cup of tea,' Ken had said, 'is what we need. It will calm us down.'

Ken rushed to the telephone. The calm voice of the Inspector came over the line. There was the feeling of laughter in his words. 'I'm taking good care of that dog of mine, and I'm taking good care of you as well. By the sound of your message you were very careful not to tell the people at the station anything.'

'Never mind about that,' said Ken, 'just listen. We've had a visitor, a visitor with a gun. You thought that someone might get in touch. Well they did. You'll have to do something to …'

Inspector West laughed. 'Calm down, calm down, you can tell me all about it tomorrow at the station.

I want you to come down there at ten o'clock to look at some people we have there.'

'What about my wife? They've said that they'll …'

'Oh, your visitor with the gun. Don't worry about him, my men picked him up as he came out of your flat. You see, we rather thought that if we got one, then the others would act. So we had someone follow you home, and he was listening outside the door. He's one of my best men, and he just took your visitor away nice and quietly. See you in the morning.'

Two months later it was all over. Ken and Mabel had forgotten the fear that they had felt. The police had caught all three bank robbers, two of them at an address that Ken had given them, the third as he left Ken's flat.

Ken had told the police all he knew, and told it again to the judge when the men were sent to prison. Then a week after that he had arrived home one evening to find Mabel very excited. 'We've just had a visitor, about the bank robbery!' she said.

'Oh no! I just want a nice quiet life. It's all over!'

'The man was from the bank.' She handed Ken an envelope. Inside was a cheque and a short note.

Ken read the note: 'To thank you for your help in catching the robbers.' His eyes fell on the cheque: 'Five thousand pounds.' He sat down, 'Let's have some tea Mabel, we need something to calm us down.'

A month after receiving the cheque Ken and Mabel stood beside a taxi while the driver put five large bags into the back.

'To the airport please, driver,' said Ken, 'and don't hurry, we have plenty of time to catch our plane.'

6

THE PARTY

The advice of friends

I do not like parties. I find them very dull and therefore try not to attend them. My friends tell me that I missed a lot of fun by not going to this or that person's party. They may be right, but I have never had any fun at the parties I have attended.

With close friends, I have tried to explain my feelings about parties, but I have not met with much success. Harold Richards, who has known about my feelings for many years, always says:

'Every party is different. You cannot talk about all parties being dull any more than you can talk about all parties being fun.

'Your trouble,' he says to me, 'is that you attend parties with the idea that you're not going to enjoy yourself, and therefore you don't enjoy yourself.'

Harold is sure that he is right. I'm sure that he's talking rubbish. When I do go to a party, I go telling myself that I must try to find out how I can enjoy standing around talking politely to people I am not really interested in, and who are usually not interested in me. I go along to try really hard to find out how other people can enjoy themselves in a crowded room, thick with cigarette smoke, where everyone drinks more than usual, talks too loudly, and behaves in a way that is very false.

I cannot enjoy what is fun for most people because (so I am told by my neighbours Victor and Betty), I'm never comfortable with strangers. 'The secret,' they have often said, 'is to have a few drinks as soon as you arrive, then you feel comfortable, and you enjoy yourself.' They may be right about this, I've never tried it simply because I dislike the idea of not being sure what I'm saying; if I have more than two drinks, then I'm not sure.

Though I listen to the advice that friends give me, I have a few ideas myself. I think that my dislike of parties is in part because I do not find it easy to talk to strangers. Then there is the question of honesty. I like to think of myself as an honest person and I dislike the way in which people behave dishonestly at parties, saying things they do not really mean, and pretending to be something they are not.

Grace Hardy, whom I've known for many years, and who is herself a great party-lover, does not agree with me on the subject of honesty. 'My dear boy,' she has often said to me, 'people aren't dishonest at parties. I go to lots of parties and I behave just the same as I do anywhere. You're talking rubbish, dear boy.' I have never been brave enough to tell Grace that she sounds dishonest all the time: one can never believe what she says. And I'm sure that she does not think of me as a 'dear boy', but that's what she always calls me.

A seat in the garden

I was thinking about all these things as I got ready to go to a party. Right up to the last minute I was fighting with myself — should I go or not? I had not told the people who invited me that I was not going, and so I felt that I should go.

When I do go to a party I am never sure if I should arrive early and feel uncomfortable if I'm the first person there, or arrive late and have everyone notice my arrival. Tonight I decided I would be early, but not too early.

When I arrived it seemed that everyone else had decided to be late. I was the first to get there. My host and hostess met me at the door. I said I was sorry to be so early. They put a drink in my hand and I was glad to see more people arriving. With attention drawn away from me by the new arrivals, I moved to the end of the room and stood looking out through the long, open windows that led to the garden. It was a warm summer evening and the open window offered me a way to get away from people when I could stand no more talk. It also meant that the cigarette smoke would not get too bad.

I was just thinking about the advantages of the open window, when I noticed out of the corner of my eye the arrival of a group of people whom I had met before. One of them was a tall man with no hair on his head but a lot under his nose, a Colonel somebody. I could not remember his name, but I remembered his loud voice and the fact that his manner frightened me and made me feel quite unable to speak.

The group was moving in my direction. I did what seemed to be the only wise thing — I stepped through the windows and into the garden. A little to one side of the windows was a garden seat. I sat down.

The seat was comfortable. The drink in my hand tasted quite pleasant. The sound of voices from the room behind me was not in any way inviting, and, to be very honest with myself, I knew that I was happier sitting there than being at the party. Any wish that I had felt before to enjoy the party had disappeared as soon as I had stepped through that window. I could not be seen from inside the room, and I prayed that no-one would decide to join me in the garden.

More people were arriving and the Colonel's group moved nearer to the window. They were only a few feet from where I was sitting and I could hear their voices quite clearly. The Colonel's voice sounded loud and clear, 'Glad I could get here, I always enjoy Charlie's parties. Interesting people.'

Charlie Rogers, my host, and his wife Helen, were not people that I knew well. I'd known them a long time but never got very close to them. They often visited Victor and Betty with whom they had been close friends for many years, and when they did so I was always invited over for a drink. Charlie never said anything interesting. Helen talked too much and too fast.

Grace Hardy had arrived. I could hear her greeting the group by the window, 'Hello dear! Wonderful to see you.' I could imagine her kissing everybody around her. I also heard Paul Chapman's voice. It was as loud as the Colonel's, but higher.

The funny little man

The room was filling up. The sound of voices was greater and I prayed again that the people would not spill out into the garden. Sitting there, I began to feel quite amused. They couldn't see me but I could hear them. I began to think that this might be one party that I would enjoy.

Then suddenly I heard someone mention my name, 'He doesn't seem to be here.' It was Victor.

'I can't think who you mean.' said the Colonel. Victor tried to explain who I was, to remind the Colonel.

The loud voice broke into laughter, 'Oh, yes, I remember him. Funny little man, doesn't speak very clearly. Not the sort that one can depend upon.'

'My dear!' it was Grace speaking. 'Let's be honest, he's dull, very very dull. I'm so glad that he's not here.'

As I have said, I've known Grace for a long time, and I was hurt by her words. But I had no time to think about my feelings. Victor started to defend me (or so it seemed at first). 'Grace that is not fair.' (Good old Victor.) 'How can you find someone dull if you don't even notice them.' Everyone laughed. I had thought Victor was a friend, but not any longer. I felt my face going red. As their laughter died away, Harold Richards was speaking, 'He hasn't come because he doesn't like parties. He's always saying so! It's as simple as that! The reason that he doesn't like parties is that he doesn't really like other people.'

'Well I agree with Grace,' said someone else. 'I'm glad he hasn't come.'

'That's the little man who never finishes a sentence, isn't it?' asked a girl that I didn't remember.

'Yes that's him,' said Paul Chapman's high voice. 'I'd say that his trouble is that he doesn't think very much of himself, that's why he's so unsure.'

'Well at least everyone agrees with him,' said someone, 'he doesn't think much of himself, and everyone agrees.' They all laughed again and I began to wish that there was a way out of the garden. If I climbed the garden wall I would end up in the garden of the next house. Then I remembered that my hat and coat were still in the house; I'd handed them to Charlie Rogers when I'd arrived.

'I'm so glad you decided to come'

The girl whose voice I couldn't remember was speaking again, 'I think you're all being very unkind to him. I think he's rather sweet.' She said the words in the way that people do when they're talking about a pet cat. But I was grateful for something.

'You think that because you don't know him as well as we do,' I heard Betty reply.

'He'd probably be all right if he'd have a few drinks,' said Victor. 'He can sit all night holding a full glass and hardly touch it.' I looked at the glass in my hand. I had drunk very little. As if to answer Victor's words I drank down the rest all at once, and put the glass on the seat beside me.

Somehow I had to get out of this garden, I'd heard enough. I stood up, being careful not to appear in front of the window. I moved round to the side of the house. The very large drink was running round inside my head. An idea was beginning to take shape. Usually I am very careful and don't act upon an idea without giving it a lot of thought. Maybe it was the drink that stopped me from thinking clearly.

By the time I had reached the front of the house my mind was made up. I would arrive again. I would simply walk in the front door, it was sure to be open. Then, as soon as possible, I'd find my hat and coat and leave.

Pushing open the front door I slipped into the hall without being noticed. There must have been fifty people in the room. The group that had been by the window were now just inside the door re-filling their glasses from the many bottles that stood on a long table by the wall.

I stopped, asking myself if I could slip past them without being noticed. Too late! They had seen me. Grace Hardy was the first to speak, 'My dear, you're so late. We were all asking where you'd got to. I'm so glad you decided to come. Let me get you a drink.'

Victor took my arm, 'Come in, old boy, it's good to see you. We were just talking about you, saying that we'd all like you to be here. Let me introduce Diana.' I took the outstretched hand of the young lady beside him. 'Diana thinks you're sweet.'

'Yes we've met before,' I said.

The Colonel shouted across the heads of the others, 'Hello old man. Glad you could come, do come and have a good long talk with me.'

I still dislike parties. When friends tell me what I'm missing, I think I'm rather glad. There are some things in life that are worth missing.

7

THE VASE

Aunt Amelia's will

Edward came into the room reading the letter. He had met the postman at the front door, opened the letter in the hall and begun reading immediately. Edward did not often receive letters which came in long brown envelopes, and he wanted to find out what it contained.

Without lifting his eyes from the letter, he sat down in the chair opposite his wife.

Emily watched Edward walk from the door to the chair, but didn't speak. She was sitting at the table, holding a cup of steaming coffee which she drank noisily. Emily never had much to say first thing in the morning, and it had been a bad night. The baby had not slept until after midnight, and then woken her with its crying at four a.m.

Edward raised his eyes, 'Listen!' he said, and began to read the letter aloud. 'You are named in the will of Mrs Amelia Hunt, who died recently. Would you please come to see the writer of this letter as soon as possible.' He stopped reading and looked up waiting for his wife to speak. Sleepily she closed her eyes and held her hand in front of her wide-open mouth. He went on, 'It's signed "James Rolf" and it's from Anderson and Rolf, Solicitors. Their office is at 59, The Causeway, London, E.C.1. The number eight bus goes near there.'

There was a short silence, then Emily looked up and asked sleepily, 'Who's Amelia Hunt?'

'Oh! you are awake,' said Edward. 'For a minute I thought I was talking to myself.' He got up, put his hands into his pockets and stood like a man about to make a speech.

'Now that I have your attention, Mrs Emily West, I would like to point out that this may be the most important letter we have ever received in our lives.' He waited for his wife to speak, but she remained silent.

Edward pulled up a chair close to Emily, took the cup from her hands, and said, 'Listen to me, Emily. Amelia Hunt may have left me a fortune, and all you can do is look sleepy.'

Emily ran a hand through her hair. She closed her eyes, opened them again, and repeated her question, 'Who's Amelia Hunt?'

'Amelia! Aunt Amelia! My Aunt Amelia. I haven't seen her since I was about ten years old. Funny old girl. She lived all alone in the country somewhere. My mother used to say that she was very rich but hid her money under the bed. She sounded a bit mad. This letter says that the old girl is dead. She may have left me all her money. This could be the answer to all our problems.'

Emily took back her cup and drank the last of her coffee. 'Why should she leave her money to you? Why you?'

'I've no idea. She may have thought I was a good little boy when I was ten years old, and she remembered me. I can't even remember what she looked like, but I'm certainly glad that she remembered me.'

'Well,' said Emily, 'you'd better go to see the solicitors and find out if we're rich. We could certainly do with some money. Sometimes I don't know how we manage, everything costs so much. We have been married nearly two years and we have not saved anything. It would be nice to be able to buy some new things.' Emily closed her eyes as soon as she stopped speaking. The Wests' baby was only a month old, and sleepless nights were already making Emily feel like an old woman.

Everything she owned

Two hours later, the letter in his hand, Edward entered the offices of Anderson and Rolf, Solicitors.

The girl behind the desk looked up as he entered, 'Good morning, sir, can I help you?' Edward handed her the letter, 'I received this letter from Mr Rolf,' he said.

The girl looked at the letter, 'Would you take a seat please, I'll see if Mr Rolf is free.' She stood up and went to the door behind her. Knocking quickly, she went in.

Edward sat waiting. He thought about how much Aunt Amelia had left him. It might only be a little, but it might be a fortune. Those family stories about Aunt Amelia's money may have been just stories, but if they had been true there should be enough money to buy a house, or Aunt Amelia may have left him her house. That would be nice. He had often thought about living in the country, and if there was enough money he would not have to look for a new job. There might be enough money to start his own business.

The office-girl returned and stood holding the door open, 'Would you come in please, Mr West.'

Mr Rolf stood up as Edward entered his office, 'It's good of you to come so quickly, Mr West. Please sit down.' He pushed a cigarette box towards Edward,

'Please smoke if you wish. A sad business, old Mrs Hunt's death, I'm so sorry.'

'Really I ...' Edward began.

But the solicitor went on.

'She was very old of course, and she had been ill for quite a long time, everyone expected it. But then you know all about that.'

'No, I didn't know,' said Edward. 'You see, I've not seen her since I was ten years old. I didn't really know her at all. In fact I was very surprised to get your letter. I can't think why she should have left me any money.' Then seeing the look of surprise on the solicitor's face, he added, 'I am her nephew of course.'

'Yes, Mr West. But I'm afraid there is no money.'

'No money?' Edward's voice rose. 'But I thought ...'

'My letter,' said Mr Rolf, 'did not say anything about money. Your aunt did leave you something, in fact she left you everything she owned.' He smiled at the puzzled look on Edward's face. 'You see, Mr West, your aunt had no money when she died. Nothing at all.'

'But I thought she was rich.'

'As far as I know your aunt was never rich, Mr West. You see she decided what she would do with her things a long time ago, in fact fifteen years ago.'

'When I was ten years old.'

'Exactly, Mr West! At that time your aunt probably did have a little money, but at the time of her death she had none at all.'

'But there's a house.'

'A house? Mr West, your aunt had no house.'

'The house where she lived. Where was it? In Kent somewhere.'

'In the village called Ash, in East Kent. That's where she lived and where she died, Mr West, but she didn't own the house, she only rented it.'

'All those old things!'

Edward saw his dream of a fortune disappearing. 'No money! No house! Then what did she leave me?'

'As I told you, Mr West, your aunt left you everything she had. In other words, she left you all the things in the house where she lived. Everything is yours.'

Edward tried to think back fifteen years. He tried to remember what Aunt Amelia's home was like. He had a memory of dusty old chairs and old pictures on the walls.

'All those old things! What am I going to do with them?'

'Well it's up to you, of course, but I think you should go down to Ash and see if there is anything there that you want. You could then take away what you wished to keep and sell what is left.' Mr Rolf put some papers on the desk in front of Edward. 'If you would just sign these papers, Mr West, then it will be all right for you to take anything you wish from your aunt's home, and to sell whatever you do not want.'

Edward looked at the papers and thought hard. 'What will happen if I don't sign these papers?' he asked.

'Then I would have to find Mrs Hunt's other relatives, and if I could not find any, I can, as her solicitor, sell the things myself. It could of course cost a lot of money to try finding her other relatives, and it could cost a lot to put the things up for sale. If the things sold for very little you might have to pay something towards the cost of the sale.'

'Yes but …'

'I do advise you to accept it, Mr West. I have not seen what is in your aunt's home, but sometimes there are things of value in the homes of old ladies like Mrs Hunt. You certainly cannot lose by it, and for a little trouble you might be a few pounds richer.'

A trip to the country

Back on the number eight bus Edward thought about what he had done. He had signed the papers in Mr Rolf's office and he had in his pocket a letter which made him the owner of 'everything in Number three, The Terrace, in the village of Ash, Kent'. He asked himself what Emily would say.

Emily took one look at his face and said, 'Bad news! She has left you five pounds and her cat.'

'Don't make jokes,' said Edward. 'Let's have a cup of tea and I'll tell you all about it.'

Emily sat with the baby in her arms listening in silence while Edward drank his tea and told her the whole story. When Edward had finished, Emily laughed. 'Don't look so unhappy,' she said. 'Mr Rolf is right. You can't lose, and you might be lucky. I think it was very sweet of your aunt to think of you. You hadn't thought about her for years until this morning, and now you're looking sad because she hasn't left you a fortune. Come on Edward, smile! It's Sunday tomorrow. We could get an early train, go down to Ash and have a look at the things. It's a good excuse to have a day out.'

By evening, Edward had got over his disappointment and was planning the next day's trip to the country. By next morning both Edward and Emily were feeling quite happy about the whole thing.

They spent the whole day in the little house in Ash, opening drawers and cupboards, sorting through old papers, and looking at old photographs that brought back half-forgotten memories. There was nothing of any great value, and very little except a few photographs that they thought worth keeping.

The Vase

They asked the neighbours to telephone a company who bought second-hand furniture and arrange the sale, and then they got ready to leave.

'If we go now,' said Emily, 'we can catch the five-thirty train back to London.'

'It does not seem right to go away without anything,' said Edward. 'We should take just a little thing to remind us of the day that we thought we had been left a fortune.'

'I know!' said Emily. 'In the back of the cupboard in the kitchen I saw some old vases. Wait for me, I'll get one.'

'Be quick or we'll miss the train.'

Emily went through to the kitchen and returned a minute later carrying something small wrapped up in newspaper.

'I've wrapped it up. Everything in the cupboard is so dirty, I don't think it's been opened for years.' She dropped it into the bag that she had used to carry the food for their lunch.

'Come on!' said Edward. 'We'll miss the train.'

The friendly passenger

They did catch the train, but only just. The guard was about to blow his whistle as they ran out onto the platform.

'Just in time!' said Edward, as they threw themselves onto the seats.

Emily sat, out of breath, still holding their lunch-bag.

There was only one other passenger. He sat opposite them, a well-dressed man with grey hair. Noting the sort of clothes that the man wore, Edward decided that he looked like a man who had spent many years as an army officer. The man had looked up as they entered the train, but was now giving all his attention to *The Sunday Times* newspaper.

'Oh!' said Edward. 'I left my newspaper at the house, I've nothing to read.'

The man opposite them looked up, 'Allow me,' he said, holding out a part of his newspaper.

'Thank you,' said Edward, 'it's very kind of you.' Then turning to Emily, he said, 'Any food left? I'm feeling hungry.'

'I think so.' Emily opened the bag and, taking out the small parcel, she placed it on the seat beside her. As she did so, the train gathered speed and the small parcel was thrown on to the floor. The man opposite reached down and only just stopped it from disappearing under the seat. As he picked it up the newspaper came away, showing the vase beneath.

'I say, I say. What have you here? Looks a very nice piece.' Emily stretched out her hand to take the vase from him. 'Would you mind very much if I had a good look at this?' he asked.

'I'm afraid it's very dirty,' said Emily. 'I didn't have time to clean it.' The man did not appear to hear her words. He was gently rubbing the dirt from part of the vase and looking closely at the pale blue colour which lay beneath. He turned it over in his hands, his fingers running around its shape. Emily went on, 'It belonged to my aunt, or rather my husband's aunt. It's just something to remember her by. There was a whole cupboard full of bits and pieces. It was the first thing I saw. I suppose it will look quite nice when it has been washed.'

The Vase

Edward joined in, 'It's probably very old. I expect it's been collecting dust in that cupboard for years. I can't think why old people keep such a lot of old rubbish. Still, as my wife says, it's just something to remember the old lady by.'

Their companion looked up, 'Yes, that's true. I take it that your aunt is dead,' he said, looking at Edward.

'Yes, she died recently and left me all the things in her house. We've just been down to the house to look at everything.'

The value of the vase

There was a short silence during which the man continued to look at the little vase. He was deep in thought. At last he looked up and, reaching into his pocket, he took out a card which he handed to Edward. 'If you ever think of selling this vase, please let me handle the sale for you.'

'Oh we wouldn't sell it,' began Emily. Edward stopped her by handing her the card. She read: 'J.T. Franks. City Sales Ltd.'

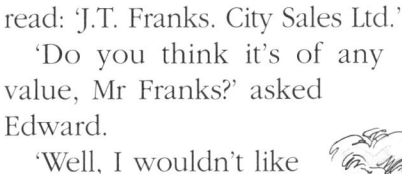

'Do you think it's of any value, Mr Franks?' asked Edward.

'Well, I wouldn't like to say without looking at it more closely. But off-hand I would say that anyone who likes to collect such things would pay quite a few pounds for it.'

At times like this Emily was always more direct than Edward, 'How much?' she asked.

Mr Franks smiled, 'Well I really wouldn't like to say how much.'

'Twenty pounds?' asked Emily.

'Well ...' began Mr Franks, but Edward stopped him.

'Emily! Mr Franks has already said that he'd rather not say. You should not have asked again.' Then turning to Mr Franks, 'Please excuse my wife.'

Though Edward appeared to be more uncomfortable about Emily's question than Mr Franks, secretly he was hoping that her question would be answered. If they could sell the vase for twenty pounds, or even more, he would certainly rather have the money than something with which to remember Aunt Amelia.

Mr Franks held up his hand, 'Don't say you're sorry, it's quite all right Mr..., I'm sorry, I don't think you told me your name.'

'West,' said Edward. 'Edward West, and my wife's name is Emily.' They all shook hands.

Mr Franks looked from one to the other, 'Mr West, Mrs West, I am in the business of selling objects like your little vase.' He weighed the vase carefully in his hands, 'This,' he continued, 'I am sure, is an object which we could sell for more than twenty pounds. If you would care to sell it, then simply call at my office and I'll arrange to have it put up for auction. That's really all there is to it.' As he finished speaking he handed the vase back to Edward.

'More than fifty pounds?' Emily said. She did not understand why Edward did not like her asking such questions.

Edward cried, 'Really, Emily!'

Mr Franks laughed, 'Yes, Mrs West, probably more than fifty pounds.'

The Vase

'We might be lucky.'

Back in their own home Edward and Emily could talk of nothing but the vase. Emily had almost forgotten to collect the baby who had been left in the care of their next-door neighbour.

'Well it doesn't look very special to me,' said Edward, turning the vase over in his hands. 'It isn't even very well made as far as I can see. There's not even a proper pattern on it. It's just plain blue with a sort of purple spot on one side.'

He stood the vase on the kitchen table. 'I'll wash it,' said Emily.

'Be careful with it,' laughed Edward, 'there's more than fifty pounds there.'

Thinking about what 'more than fifty' really meant, Edward made his way next morning to the offices of City Sales Ltd. 'More than fifty could mean sixty, seventy, or even a hundred,' he thought. He had thought earlier that morning that any amount more than fifty pounds was a good reason for taking the morning off work, and at eight-thirty Emily had telephoned his office with a false story about a bad stomach pain.

Mr Frank's office was full of dusty looking papers. He took a large bundle of them from a chair on which he invited Edward to sit. 'Would you like some coffee, Mr West?' He pressed a switch on the brown wooden box beside him and lowered his head towards it, 'Coffee for my visitor please, Mary.'

'Now, Mr West, I must tell you that if I put your little vase up for auction, neither my company nor myself can be sure about its safety. We cannot be sure how much money will be paid for it, either. We do take the best care that we can, and we do try to get the best price possible. We take ten per cent, so the better the price we get for you, the more we earn for ourselves.'

Edward said that he understood and put the little vase on the desk in front of Mr West. Just then a girl entered carrying two cups of coffee.

'You'd like to sell then, Mr West?'

'Yes, why not?' answered Edward. 'We might be lucky.'

'Yes, as you say, you might be lucky,' said Mr Franks. Edward watched as the other man wrote on a piece of paper. 'It's necessary, you understand, to have this in writing. It gives us your permission to sell.' He pressed the switch again, 'Would you come please, Mary.'

The girl came in and Mr Franks handed her the note, 'Type this out please, Mary. Two copies.'

The day of the auction

During the four weeks that followed Edward's visit to Mr Franks, the Wests seemed to change. Edward had received the money from the second-hand furniture people in Ash. It was three hundred pounds, which was much more than he had expected, and more than the Wests had ever had at one time before.

Emily had wanted to spend it on the house. 'There are so many things we need,' she had said.

Edward wanted to save it, 'Put it in the bank and forget about it. It's nice to have something saved.'

They had quarrelled.

'With all this money,' Emily had said, 'I wish that we had not agreed to sell that vase. It would have been nice to have kept it. We will only get fifty pounds which is not really very much.'

'I wish you'd stop talking about the vase' had been Edward's reply whenever his wife spoke of it.

The Vase

They had quarrelled again. They both became angry very easily. They were both waiting for the day of the auction.

'I'll be glad when it's over,' said Edward. 'I wish I'd never seen the vase. And I'm not taking time off work to go to the auction. You can go if you wish!'

On the morning of the auction neither Edward nor Emily had spoken of it. Both were thinking, but neither spoke. When Edward was safely off to work, Emily began to dress the baby ready for the journey. She had made up her mind that nothing would stop her from attending the auction. If it had been possible she would have gone alone, but she could not find anyone to look after the baby.

Leaving the house, she hurried towards the end of the road just in time to see a bus starting off from the bus stop. She waved at the driver, but he drove straight past. This made her angry, but she told herself that she must simply be patient. Sometimes there was a long wait between buses and she did not want to miss the start of the auction.

Fifteen minutes later, fifteen minutes that seemed twice as long to Emily, she saw another bus appear in the distance. As she saw it the baby gave a loud cry and was sick.

Poor Emily, she was so angry she could have cried. There was nothing she could do but go home. She hated the idea of missing the auction.

There are times when a mother's love for her baby is put to the test. For Emily this was one of those times. Even though her love for her baby was at that moment not as great as usual, she carefully undressed, washed, and re-dressed the baby in clean clothes. Then looking at the clock she thought again about going to the auction to see the vase being sold. She decided to try.

'Selling at forty-five'

Emily had not been to an auction before. She was surprised to find about fifty people there, seated in rows in front of the auctioneer. The only sound was the auctioneer's voice, 'Eighteen, nineteen, twenty, twenty-one. Will anyone give me twenty-one?'

The auctioneer's table stood on a small platform at one end of the room. On the floor in front of the platform stood another man. In his hand, held so that everyone could see it, was the little blue vase. She was just in time!

As the vase was held up, Emily felt proud. A man seated just in front of her lifted his finger. The auctioneer noticed him, 'Twenty-one at the back, twenty-one, thank you, sir.'

'More than twenty,' thought Emily. The baby, asleep in her arms, began to move. Emily looked down and prayed that it wouldn't wake.

Someone in the front spoke softly. Emily could not catch the words, but the auctioneer had heard. 'Thirty,' he said.

The man in front of her lifted his finger again. 'Thirty-one,' said the auctioneer. 'More than thirty,' thought Emily. The baby began to make little noises, those little noises that every mother knows will soon become louder. One or two heads turned in Emily's direction, their owners wanted to hear the auctioneer, not Emily's baby.

As the auctioneer was saying, 'Thirty-five, who'll make it forty?' the baby began to cry loudly. All heads turned. The auctioneer removed his glasses and looked over the heads of his audience, 'Madam, would you mind?'

Motherly love was being tested again. Emily rose and walked out into the hall. The doorman closed the door behind her. Taking a seat in the hall, Emily reached into the large handbag in which she carried all those many things that are important to the comfort of a baby. From it she took a feeding-bottle with some warm milk in it. Between cries the baby sucked at the bottle, and two minutes later was fast asleep.

With her motherly love growing stronger Emily opened the door of the auction room a little. The auctioneer's voice sounded loud and clear, 'Forty-five. Selling at forty-five, going, going, gone!'

Very lucky people

On the way home on the bus Emily took comfort in the thought that she and Edward were really very lucky people. They had a lovely baby, and they had three hundred pounds in the bank and another forty-five to come. 'Less ten per cent,' she said to herself.

Mr Franks had said 'probably more than fifty pounds' but all the same they were very lucky.

By the time Edward arrived home that night the baby was in bed and Emily had laid food ready on the kitchen table. Edward kissed her. 'Did you go?' There was no need for him to say where. Secretly they had both hoped that the vase would sell for more than fifty pounds. Emily knew he would be disappointed.

'Yes I went.'

'How much?'

'Forty-five. Don't be disappointed, we have got the other money.'

When you are young and have a loving wife, a lovely baby, and three hundred pounds in the bank, it's hard to stay disappointed for very long. Edward soon got over it.

A week later Edward came into the room with a letter in his hand. He had met the postman at the front door. The letter was in a long brown envelope, but this time he could guess what it was. He walked into the kitchen where Emily was sitting half-asleep, she had had another bad night with the baby. She looked up as he entered, 'Post?'

'Yes,' he said, and threw the envelope down on to the kitchen table. 'It will be the cheque from City Sales.'

Emily opened it and looked at the short note inside. Edward picked up the cheque. Emily read the words in silence: 'Sale by auction of one small blue Chinese Sung vase. Sold for forty-five thousand pounds.'

She looked up at Edward. He sat, cheque in hand, staring straight in front of him. 'Let's have a cup of tea, Emily,' he said.

QUESTIONS AND ACTIVITIES

CHAPTER 1 (A)

Choose the right words to say what this part of the story is about.

Polly left work (1) **late/early** because of the fog. The fog was so (2) **thick/thin** that there were no buses to Crouch End. Polly took an Underground (3) **bus/train** to Finsbury Park which was two (4) **metres/miles** from her home. When she was waiting for the train she saw a (5) **tall/short** man in a dark (6) **hat/coat** looking at her. On the train Polly noticed that he was still watching her. When she got (7) **off/on** the train she saw him (8) **behind/in front of** her on the stairs.

CHAPTER 1 (B)

*Use these words to fill the gaps: **silence, train, decided, voice, cough, footsteps, doorway, tapping.***

Polly (1) ____ to walk home through the fog. It was very difficult. She heard (2) ____ coming from behind her. When she stopped to listen, there was complete (3) ____. She thought she saw someone step into a shop (4) ____.

Then she heard a soft footstep and a deep (5) ____. She heard a strange (6) ____ noise quite close to her. Then someone spoke to her in a deep (7) ____. She found herself looking up at a tall man, but it was not the man she had seen in the (8) ____.

CHAPTER 2

Put the letters of these words in the right order. The first one is 'library'.

Tom sat in the (1) **brilyar**, trying to study. He closed his eyes, but he didn't fall (2) **palese**. When he opened them, he saw an old man (3) **tignist** in front of him. The old man told Tom about Greek (4) **tyroish**. He spoke in a very (5) **nestigniter** way. The old man's face was (6) **nidle** and grey, but his eyes were (7) **gunoy** eyes. When he left, Tom started looking at the (8) **strupice** in the book. He found one that looked just like the old man. It was of a Greek man called (9) **Astoliter**.

CHAPTER 3 (A)

Which of these statements are true, and which are false? What is wrong with the false ones?

1 Sir Nathaniel Marks was a very poor man.
2 He asked to borrow one thousand pounds from the bank.
3 Henry thought Sir Nathaniel was joking.
4 He said the bank would take his cheque for any amount.
5 Mr Bromley forgot about the letter from Head Office.
6 He thought he had better keep Sir Nathaniel happy.
7 He agreed to let Sir Nathaniel lend him the money.
8 Sir Nathaniel said there was no need to sign the forms.
9 He made Mr Bromley take his car to keep it safe.

CHAPTER 3 (B)

Put the right endings with the right beginnings.

1 A month later, Sir Nathaniel …
2 He returned the money,
3 He had borrowed the money …
4 The bet was to keep his car …
5 This must cost him …
6 For one month, the car was …
7 It had cost him nothing …
8 The loan had only cost him …
9 So Sir Nathaniel …

(a) won his bet.
(b) in a garage for a month.
(c) to keep it there.
(d) and took his car.
(e) forty-two pence.
(f) less than fifty pence.
(g) because of a bet.
(h) in the bank's garage.
(i) came back to the bank.

QUESTIONS AND ACTIVITIES

CHAPTER 4

Put what Nicholas said in the correct boxes:

They said:	Nicholas said:
1 His mother asked him if he would like to come in.	(a) that it would take too long to explain.
2 Miss Marchant asked him what he was playing.	(b) 'No, thank you!'
3 Miss Marchant asked him what he was building.	(c) that old ladies never understood what he did.
4 His mother told him to apologize to Miss Marchant.	(d) that he was building something.

CHAPTER 5

Put the underlined sentences in the right paragraphs.

1 Inspector West asked Ken to go to the police station. <u>That meant somebody who had handled the handkerchief had been in Ken's taxi that day.</u> He asked Ken to think about the passengers he had had.

2 The taxi had been washed the night before. <u>Then they let Ken go back to work.</u> So one of Ken's passengers must be connected with the bank robbery.

3 The police checked the taxi for finger prints. <u>He wanted Ken to answer a few questions.</u> Inspector West told Ken to telephone him if anyone got in touch with him.

Chapter 6

Put these sentences in the right order. The first one is correct. (The narrator is the person who tells the story.)

1 The narrator had been sitting in the garden alone.
2 Everyone said they were glad that he had come.
3 He went round the side of the house to the front door.
4 She had been saying quite nice things about him.
5 He did not like what they said.
6 They introduced him to Diana.
7 He arrived at the party for a second time.
8 He heard some people in the house talking about him.
9 He decided to leave, but he had to get his hat and coat.

Chapter 7 (A)

Use these words to fill the gaps: **lived, solicitor, house, will, owned, rented, money, died.**

Edward West's aunt Amelia died. In her (1) ____ she left him all that she (2) ____. Edward thought his aunt might have left him some money, or her house, but the (3) ____, Mr Rolf, told Edward that his aunt had had no (4) ____ when she (5) ____. He also said she did not own the house where she (6) ____, she only (7) ____ it. Edward was not very happy because he would only get all the old things in the (8) ____.

Chapter 7 (B)

Copy the table and put the missing words in the right places. Choose from: **kitchen, remind, cupboard, thousand, cheque, train, vase, anyone, auctioneer, collected, fortune.**

At Ash, Emily saw an old (1) ____ in the (2) ____ (3) ____. She took it to (4) ____ them of the day they thought they had been left a (5) ____. Going home on the (6) ____, they met Mr Franks. He thought (7) ____ who (8) ____ old things might like to buy the vase. At the auction, Emily thought the (9) ____ had sold the vase for forty-five pounds, but a week later Edward received a (10) ____ for forty-five (11) ____ pounds.

Questions and Activities 89

GRADE 1

Alice's Adventures in Wonderland
Lewis Carroll

The Call of the Wild and Other Stories
Jack London

Emma
Jane Austen

The Golden Goose and Other Stories
Retold by David Foulds

Jane Eyre
Charlotte Brontë

Little Women
Louisa M. Alcott

The Lost Umbrella of Kim Chu
Eleanor Estes

Tales From the Arabian Nights
Edited by David Foulds

Treasure Island
Robert Louis Stevenson

GRADE 2

The Adventures of Sherlock Holmes
Sir Arthur Conan Doyle

A Christmas Carol
Charles Dickens

The Dagger and Wings and Other Father Brown Stories
G.K. Chesterton

The Flying Heads and Other Strange Stories
Edited by David Foulds

The Golden Touch and Other Stories
Edited by David Foulds

Gulliver's Travels — A Voyage to Lilliput
Jonathan Swift

The Jungle Book
Rudyard Kipling

Life Without Katy and Other Stories
O. Henry

Lord Jim
Joseph Conrad

A Midsummer Night's Dream and Other Stories from Shakespeare's Plays
Edited by David Foulds

Oliver Twist
Charles Dickens

The Prince and the Pauper
Mark Twain

The Stone Junk and Other Stories
D.H. Howe

Stories from Shakespeare's Comedies
Retold by Katherine Mattock

The Talking Tree and Other Stories
David McRobbie

Through the Looking Glass
Lewis Carroll

GRADE 3

The Adventures of Tom Sawyer
Mark Twain

Around the World in Eighty Days
Jules Verne

The Canterville Ghost and Other Stories
Oscar Wilde

David Copperfield
Charles Dickens

Fog and Other Stories
Bill Lowe

Further Adventures of Sherlock Holmes
Sir Arthur Conan Doyle

Great Expectations
Charles Dickens